# TWO OR THREE GRACES

# By Aldous Huxley

℃ *Novels*
> THOSE BARREN LEAVES
> ANTIC HAY
> CROME YELLOW

℃ *Short Stories*
> LITTLE MEXICAN
> MORTAL COILS
> LIMBO

℃ *Essays*
> ALONG THE ROAD
> ON THE MARGIN

℃ *Poetry*
> LEDA

℃ *Drama*
> THE DISCOVERY, *adapted from Frances Sheridan*

# TWO OR THREE GRACES

## AND OTHER STORIES

*By*

# ALDOUS HUXLEY

LONDON

CHATTO & WINDUS

1926

# CONTENTS

∽

# TWO OR THREE
# GRACES

THE word 'bore' is of doubtful etymology.
Some authorities derive it from the verb meaning to pierce.   A bore is a person who drills
a hole in your spirit, who tunnels relentlessly
through your patience, through all the crusts
of voluntary deafness, inattention, rudeness,
which you vainly interpose—through and
through till he pierces to the very quick of
your being.   But there are other authorities,
as good or even better, who would derive
the word from the French *bourrer*, to stuff,
to satiate.   If this etymology be correct, a
bore is one who stuffs you with his thick and
suffocating discourse, who rams his suety personality, like a dumpling, down your throat.
He stuffs you ;  and you, to use an apposite
modern metaphor, are 'fed up with him.'   I
like to think, impossibly, that both these
derivations of the word are correct ;  for bores
are both piercers and stuffers.   They are like
dentists' drills, and they are also like stale
buns.   But they are characterized by a further
quality, which drills and dough-nuts do not
possess ;  they cling.   That is why (though
no philologist) I venture to suggest a third
derivation, from 'burr.'   Burr, *bourrer*, bore—

A                    I

all the sticking, stuffing, piercing qualities of boredom are implicit in those three possible etymologies. Each of the three of them deserves to be correct.

Herbert Comfrey was above all a sticking bore. He attached himself to any one who had the misfortune to come in contact with him; attached himself and could not be shaken off. A burr-bore, vegetable and passive; not actively penetrating. For Herbert, providentially, was not particularly talkative; he was too lazy and lymphatic for that. He was just exceedingly sociable, like a large sentimental dog that cannot bear to be left alone. Like a dog, he followed people about ; he lay, metaphorically speaking, at their feet in front of the fire. And like a dog, he did not talk. It was just your company that made him happy ; he was quite content if he might trot at your side or doze under your chair. He did not demand that you should pay much attention to him ; all that he asked was to be permitted to enjoy the light of your countenance and bask in the warmth of your presence. If once a week he got the equivalent of a pat on the head and a ' Good dog, Herbert,' he wagged his spirit's tail and was perfectly happy.

To some of my friends—the quick, the impatient, the highly strung—poor vegetable Herbert was exasperating to the point of madness. His very virtues—that good nature of

his, that placidity, that unshakable fidelity—
infuriated them. Even his appearance drove
them wild. The sight of his broad smiling face,
of his big, lazy, lubberly body and limbs was
alone sufficient to set their nerves twittering and
jumping like a frightened aviary. I have known
people who, after living in the same house with
Herbert for three days, have secretly packed
their trunks, caught the first convenient train,
and, leaving no address, have travelled hundreds
of miles in order to escape from him.

To me, poor Herbert was boring indeed,
but not exasperatingly or intolerably so.
Mine is a patient temper ; my nerves are
not easily set twittering. I even liked him
in a way ; he was such a good, faithful, kind
old dog. And I soon acquired, in his dumb
presence, a knack of quite ignoring him, of
regarding him simply as a piece of furniture
—so much so, that I sometimes caught
myself on the point of carelessly setting down
my emptied coffee-cup on his head as he sat
on the floor beside me (he always sat on the
floor whenever it was possible), or of flicking
my cigarette ash into the inviting cranny
between his neck and his coat collar.

As boys, Herbert and I had been at the
same public school. But as we were in
different houses and he was two years older
than I (two years, at that age, is an enormous
seniority), we had hardly ever spoken to one

3

another. But none the less, it was on the strength of our old school that Herbert re-introduced himself into my life. His return was doubly disastrous. A bore entered my existence and, in the entering, drove out, temporarily at least, a being who, whatever his other qualities, was the very antithesis of boredom.

It was in a café of the Passage du Panorama in Paris that the thing happened. We had been sitting there for an hour, Kingham and I, talking and drinking vermouth. It was characteristic of Kingham that he did most of both—drinking as well as talking. Characteristic, too, that he should have been abusing me, among many other things, for wasting my time and spirit in precisely these two occupations.

' You sit about,' he said, ' letting every thought in your head trickle out uselessly in talk. Not that there are many thoughts, of course, because you daren't think. You do anything not to think. You create futile business, you rush about seeing people you don't like and don't take the slightest interest in, you drift from bar to bar, you swill till you're stupefied—all because you daren't think and can't bring yourself to make the effort to do something serious and decent. It's the result partly of laziness, partly of lack of faith—faith in anything. *Garçon !* ' He

4

ordered another vermouth. ' It 's the great modern vice,' he went on, ' the great temptation of every young man or woman who 's intelligent and acutely conscious. Everything that 's easy and momentarily diverting and anaesthetic tempts—people, chatter, drink, fornication. Everything that 's difficult and big, everything that needs thought and effort, repels. It 's the war that did it. Not to mention the peace. But it would have come gradually in any case. Modern life was making it inevitable. Look at the young people who had nothing to do with the war— were only children when it happened—they 're the worst of all. It 's time to stop, it 's time to do something. Can't you see that you can't go on like this ? Can't you see ? '

He leaned across the table at me, angrily. He hated these vices which he had attributed to me, hated them with a special fury because they happened really to be his. He was confessing the weakness he hated in himself —hated and could not eradicate.

Kingham looked handsome in anger. He had dark eyes, beautiful and very bright ; his hair was dark brown, fine and plentiful; a close-cut beard, redder than his hair, disguised the lower part of his face, with whose pale, young smoothness it seemed curiously incongruous. There was a brilliancy, a vividness about him. If I were less slow to kindle, I should have burned

5

responsively with his every ardour. Being what
I am, I could always remain cool, critical, and
cautious, however passionately he might burn.
My uninflammableness, I believe, had somehow fascinated him. I exasperated him, but he
continued to frequent my company—chiefly
to abuse me, to tell me passionately how hopeless I was. I winced under these dissections ;
for though he often talked, as far as I was
concerned, wildly at random (accusing me,
as he had done on this particular occasion,
of the weakness which he felt and resented in
himself), his analysis was often painfully exact
and penetrating. I winced, but all the same I
delighted in his company. We irritated one
another profoundly ; but we were friends.

I suppose I must have smiled at Kingham's
question. Goodness knows, I am no tee-
totaller, I am not averse to wasting my time
over agreeable futilities. But compared with
Kingham—particularly the Kingham of 1920
—I am a monument of industry, dutiful
steadiness, sobriety. I take no credit to
myself for it ; I happen to be one of nature's
burgesses, that is all. I am as little capable
of leading a perfectly disorderly life as I am
of, shall we say, writing a good book. Kingham was born with both talents. Hence the
absurdity, so far as I was concerned, of his
hortatory question. I did not mean to smile ;
but some trace of my amusement must have

appeared on my face, for Kingham suddenly
became most passionately angry.

'You think it's a joke?' he cried, and
thumped the marble table. 'I tell you,
it's the sin against the Holy Ghost. It's
unforgivable. It's burying your talent.
Damn this blasted Bible,' he added with
parenthetic fury. 'Why is it that one can
never talk about anything serious without
getting mixed up in it?'

'It happens to be quite a serious book,' I
suggested.

'A lot you understand about it,' said Kingham. 'I tell you,' he went on impressively.
. . . But at this moment Herbert made his
second entry into my life.

I felt a hand laid on my shoulder, looked
up, and saw a stranger.

'Hullo, Wilkes,' said the stranger. 'You
don't remember me.'

I looked more attentively, and had to admit
that I didn't.

'I am Comfrey,' he explained, 'Herbert
Comfrey. I was at Dunhill's, don't you
remember? You were at Struthers', weren't
you? Or was it Lane's?'

At the names of these pedagogues, who
had figured so largely in my boyhood, recesses
in my mind, long closed, suddenly burst open,
as though before a magical word. Visions
of inky schoolrooms, football fields, cricket

fields, fives courts, the school chapel, rose up confusedly ; and from the midst of this educational chaos there disengaged itself the loutish figure of Comfrey of Dunhill's.

'Of course,' I said, and took him by the hand. Through the corner of my eye, I saw Kingham angrily frowning. 'How did you remember me ? '

'Oh, I remember every one,' he answered. It was no vain boast, as I afterwards discovered; he *did* remember. He remembered every one he had ever met, and all the trivial incidents of his past life. He had the enormous memory of royal personages and family re-tainers—the memory of those who never read, or reason, or reflect, and whose minds are therefore wholly free to indulge in retro-spect. 'I never forget a face,' he added, and without being invited, sat down at our table.

Indignantly, Kingham threw himself back in his chair. He kicked me under the table. I looked at him and made a little grimace, signifying my helplessness.

I mumbled a perfunctory introduction. Kingham said nothing, only frowned more blackly, as he shook hands with Herbert. And for his part, Herbert was hardly more cordial. True, he smiled his amiable dim smile ; but he said nothing, he hardly even looked at Kingham. He was in too much of a hurry to turn back to me and talk about

8

the dear old school. The dear old school—
it was the only subject that ever made Herbert
really loquacious. It metamorphosed him
from a merely vegetable burr-bore into an
active, piercing dentist's drill of tediousness.
He had a passion for the school, and thought
that all ex-members of it ought to be in
constant and friendly communication with
one another. I have noticed that, as a general
rule, people of decided individuality very
rarely continue their schoolboy acquaintance-
ships into later life. It is only to be expected.
The chances that they will have found in
the tiny microcosm of school the sort of
friends they will like when they are grown
up—grown out of recognition—are obviously
very small. Coteries whose bond of union
consists in the fact that their component
members happened to be at the same school
at the same time are generally the dreariest
of assemblages. It could scarcely be otherwise ; men who have no better reasons for
associating with one another must be colourless
indeed, and insipid. Poor Herbert, who
regarded the accident of our having worn
similarly striped caps and blazers at a certain
period of our boyhood as being a sufficient
reason for our entering into a bosom friendship, was only an extreme specimen of the
type.

I put on my chilliest and most repellant

manner. But in vain. Herbert talked and
talked. Did I remember the exciting match
against Winchester in 1910? And how
poor old Mr. Cutler had been ragged? And
that memorable occasion when Pye had climbed
on to the roof of the school chapel, at night,
and hung a chamber-pot on one of the Gothic
pinnacles? Anxiously, I looked towards
Kingham. He had exchanged his expression
of anger for one of contempt, and was leaning
back, his eyes shut, tilting his chair.

Kingham had never been to a public
school. He had not had the luck (or the
misfortune) to be born a hereditary, professional gentleman. He was proud of the
fact, he sometimes even boasted of it. But
that did not prevent him from being morbidly
sensitive to anything that might be interpreted
as a reference to his origin. He was always
on the look-out for insults from ' gentlemen.'
Veiled insults, insults offered unconsciously
even, unintentionally, in perfect ignorance—
any sort of insult was enough to set him
quivering with pain and fury. More than
once I had seen him take violent offence at
words that were entirely well-intentioned.
Would he regard Herbert's dreary recollections of the dear old school as an insult?
He was quite capable of it. I looked forward
nervously to an outburst and a violent exit.
But the scene, this time, was not to be acted

in public. After listening for a few minutes
to Herbert's anecdotage, Kingham got up,
excused himself with ironical politeness, and
bade us good evening. I laid my hand on
his arm.

' Do stay.'

' A thousand regrets ' ; he laid his hand
on his heart, smiled, bowed, and was gone,
leaving me (I may add parenthetically that
it was his habit) to pay for his drinks.

We public school men were left to ourselves.

The next morning I lay late in bed. At
about eleven o'clock Kingham burst into my
room. The scene which I had been spared
the night before was enacted for me now
with redoubled passion. Another man would
have slept on the supposed insult and, waking,
have found it negligible. Not so Kingham.
He had brooded over his wrongs, till what
was originally small had grown enormous.
The truth was that Kingham liked scenes.
He loved to flounder in emotion—his own
and other people's. He was exhilarated by
these baths of passion ; he felt that he really
lived, that he was more than a man, while
he splashed about in them. And the in-
toxication was so delicious that he indulged
in it without considering the consequences—
or perhaps it would be truer to say that he
considered the consequences (for intellectually

no man could be clearer-sighted than Kingham) but deliberately ignored them.

When I say that he had a great facility
for making scenes, I do not mean to imply
that he ever simulated an emotion. He
felt genuinely about things—genuinely and
strongly, but too easily. And he took
pleasure in cultivating and working up his
emotions. For instance, what in other men
would have been a passing irritation, held
in check by self-control, to be modified very
likely by subsequent impressions, was con-
verted by Kingham, almost deliberately, into
a wild fury which no second thoughts were
allowed to assuage. Often these passions
were the result of mere mistakes on the
part of those who had provoked them. But
once emotionally committed, Kingham would
never admit a mistake—unless, of course,
his passion for self-humiliation happened at
the moment to be stronger than his passion
for self-assertion. Often, too, he would take
up unchanging emotional attitudes towards
people. A single powerful impression would
be allowed to dominate all other impressions.
His intellect was put into blinkers, the most
manifest facts were ignored ; and until further
orders the individual in question produced
in Kingham only one particular set of reactions.

As he approached my bed, I could see from

the expression on his white face that I was in for a bad quarter of an hour.

' Well ? ' I said, with an affectation of careless cordiality.

' I always knew you were an intellectual snob,' Kingham began in a low, intense voice, drawing up a chair to my bedside as he spoke. ' But really, I thought you were above being an ordinary, suburban, lower middle-class social snob.'

I made the grimace which in French novels is represented by the sign ' —— ? '

' I know that my father was a plumber,' he went on, ' and that I was educated at the expense of the State and by scholarships for the encouragement of clever paupers. I know I speak Cockney, and not Eton and Oxford. I know that my manners are bad and that I eat dirtily, and that I don't wash my teeth enough.' (None of these things were true ; but it suited Kingham, at the moment, to believe that they were. He wanted to feel abased, in order that he might react with greater violence. He insulted himself in order that he might attribute the insults, under which he genuinely winced, to me, and so have an excuse for being angry with me.) ' I know I 'm a cad and a little bounder.' He spoke the words with an extraordinary gusto, as though he enjoyed the pain he was inflicting on himself. ' I know I 'm an outsider, only tolerated for my

cleverness.   A sort of buffoon or tame monkey
for the amusement of cultured gentlemen.
I know all this, and I know you knew it.   But
I really thought you didn't mind, that we
met as human beings, not as specimens of
upper and lower classes.   I was fool enough
to imagine that you liked me in spite of it all.
I thought you even preferred me to the people
in your own herd.   It only shows what an
innocent I am.   No sooner does a gentleman
come along, an old school chum, what ? '
(derisively he assumed the public school
accent as rendered on the music hall stage)
' than you fling your arms round his neck
and leave the dirty little outsider very definitely
outside.'   He laughed ferociously.

' My good Kingham,' I began, ' why will
you make a bloody fool of yourself ? '

But Kingham, who doubtless knew as well
as I did that he was making a fool of himself,
only went on with the process more vehe-
mently.   He was committed to making a
fool of himself, and he liked it.   Shifting his
ground a little, he began telling me home
truths—real home truths this time.   In the
end, I too began to get angry.

' I 'll trouble you to get out,' I said.

' Oh, I 've not finished yet.'

' And stay out till you 've got over your
fit of hysterics.   You 're behaving like a girl
who needs a husband.'

'As I was saying,' Kingham went on in a voice that had become softer, more sinisterly quiet, more poisonously honied in proportion as mine had grown louder and harsher, 'your great defect is spiritual impotence. Your morality, your art—they're just impotence organized into systems. Your whole view of life—impotence again. Your very strength, such as it is—your horrible passive resistance —that's based in impotence too.'

'Which won't prevent me from throwing you downstairs if you don't clear out at once.' It is one thing to know the truth about oneself; it is quite another thing to have it told one by somebody else. I knew myself a natural bourgeois; but when Kingham told me so—and in his words—it seemed to me that I was learning a new and horribly unpleasant truth.

'Wait,' Kingham drawled out with exasperating calm, 'wait one moment. One more word before I go.'

'Get out,' I said. 'Get out at once.'

There was a knock at the door. It opened. The large, ruddy face of Herbert Comfrey looked round it into the room.

'I hope I don't disturb,' said Herbert, grinning at us.

'Oh, not a bit, not a bit,' cried Kingham. He jumped up, and with an excessive politeness proffered his vacant chair. 'I was just

15

going. Do sit down. Wilkes was impatiently expecting you. Sit down, do sit down.'
He propelled Herbert towards the chair.

' Really,' Herbert began, politely protesting.
But Kingham cut him short. ' And now
I leave you two old friends together,' he said.
' Good-bye. Good-bye. I 'm only sorry I
shan't have an opportunity for saying that
last word I wanted to say.'

Cumbrously, Herbert made as though to
get up. ' I 'll go,' he said. ' I had no idea.
. . . I 'm so sorry.'

But Kingham put his hands on his shoulders
and forced him back into the chair. ' No, no,'
he insisted. ' Stay where you are. I 'm off.'

And picking up his hat, he ran out of the
room.

' Queer fellow,' said Herbert. 'Who is he?'

' Oh, a friend of mine,' I answered. My
anger had dropped, and I wondered, sadly,
whether in calling him a friend I was telling
the truth. And to think that, if he were no
longer my friend, it was because of this
lumpish imbecile sitting by my bed ! I
looked at Herbert pensively. He smiled at
me—a smile that was all good nature. One
could not bear a grudge against such a man.

The breach was complete, at any rate for
the time ; it was more than two years before
Kingham and I met again. But if I had lost
Kingham, I had acquired Herbert Comfrey

—only too completely. From that moment, my life in Paris was no longer my own ; I had to share it with Herbert. Being at that moment quite unattached, a dog without a master, he fastened himself to me, taking it ingenuously for granted that I would be just as happy in his company as he was in mine. He established himself in my hotel, and for the rest of my stay in Paris I was almost never alone. I ought, I know, to have been firm with Herbert ; I ought to have been rude, told him to go to the devil, kicked him downstairs. But I lacked the heart. I was too kind. (Another symptom of my spiritual impotence ! My morality— impotence systematized. I know, I know.) Herbert preyed on me, and, like the Brahman who permits himself, unresistingly, to be devoured by every passing blood-sucker, from mosquitoes to tigers, I suffered him to prey on me. The most I did was occasionally to run away from him. Herbert was, fortunately, a sluggard. The Last Trump would hardly have got him out of bed before ten. When I wanted a day's freedom, I ordered an eight-o'clock breakfast and left the hotel while Herbert was still asleep. Returning at night from these holidays, I would find him waiting, dog-like, in my room. I always had the impression that he had been waiting there the whole day—from dawn (or what for him

was dawn—about noon) to midnight. And
he was always so genuinely pleased to see me
back that I was almost made to feel ashamed,
as though I had committed an act of perfidy.
I would begin to apologize and explain.
I had had to go out early to see a man about
something ; and then I had met another man,
who had asked me to have lunch with him ;
and then I had had to go to my dear old
friend, Madame Dubois, for tea ; after which
I had dropped in on Langlois, and we had dined
and gone to a concert. In fine, as he could see,
I could not have got back a minute earlier.

It was in answer to the reproaches of my
own conscience that I made these apologies.
Poor Herbert never complained ; he was only
too happy to see me back. I could not help
feeling that his clinging fidelity had established
some sort of claim on me, that I was somehow
a little responsible for him. It was absurd,
of course, unreasonable and preposterous.
For why should I, the victim, feel pity for
my persecutor ? Preposterous ; and yet the
fact remained that I did feel pity for him.
I have always been too tender-hearted, in-
sufficiently ruthless.

The time came for me to return to London.
Herbert, who had just enough money to
make it unnecessary for him to do anything
or to be anywhere at any particular time,
packed his bags and got into the same train.

It was a very disagreeable journey ; the train was crowded, the sea just choppy enough to make me sick.   Coming on deck as we drew into Dover harbour, I found Herbert looking exasperatingly well.   If I had not been feeling so ill, I should have found an excuse for quarrelling with him.   But I had not the requisite energy.   Meanwhile, it must be admitted, Herbert made himself very useful about the luggage.

Experience was shortly to teach me that, instead of feeling exasperated with poor Herbert, I ought to have been thankful that he was not far worse.   For Herbert, after all, was only a burr-bore, a passive vegetable clinger.   I might have been fastened on by one who was actively and piercingly as well as just clingingly boring.   Herbert might, for example, have been like his brother-in-law, John Peddley ;  and then there would have been only three alternatives left me :  murder, suicide, exile.   I was feeling annoyed with Herbert as we slid slowly across Dover harbour.   A few hours later, I had realized that I ought to have been feeling thankful that he was no worse than he was.   On Dover quay we met John Peddley.

Peddley was an active bore, the most active, I think, that I ever met ;  an indefatigable piercer, a relentless stuffer and crammer. He talked incessantly, and his knowledge of

uninteresting subjects was really enormous.
All that I know of the Swiss banking system,
of artificial manures, of the law relating to
insurance companies, of pig-breeding, of the
ex-sultan of Turkey, of sugar rationing during
the war, and a hundred other similar subjects,
is due to Peddley. He was appalling, really
appalling ; there is no other word. I know
no human being with whom I would less
willingly pass an hour.

And yet the man was extremely amiable
and full of good qualities. He had a kind
heart. He was energetic and efficient. He
was even intelligent. One could not listen
to his account of insurance companies or
artificial manures without realizing that he
had completely mastered his subject. Moreover, a successful solicitor, like Peddley,
cannot be a fool ; at least, that is what those
of us who are not solicitors like to believe.
What made the man so afflicting was his
genius for dulness ; his self-assertive pedantry ;
his voice ; his highly developed social instinct ; and finally his insensitiveness. His
genius for dulness caused him unfailingly to
take an interest in the things which interested nobody else ; and even when, by some
mistake, he embarked on some more promising
theme than the Swiss banking system, he had
the power of rendering the most intrinsically
fascinating of subjects profoundly dull. By

a process of inverse alchemy he transmuted the purest gold to lead. His self-assertiveness and a certain pedagogic instinct made him ambitious to be the instructor of his fellows ; he loved the sound of his own lecturing voice. And what a voice ! Not unmusical, but loud, booming, persistent. It set up strange, nay, positively dangerous vibrations in one's head. I could never listen to it for more than a few minutes without feeling confused and dizzy. If I had had to live with that voice, I believe I should have begun, one day, to turn and turn like those Japanese waltzing mice—for ever. Peddley's voice affected the semi-circular canals. And then there was his sociability. It was a passion, a vice ; he could not live without the company of his fellow-beings. It was an agony for him to be alone. He hunted company ferociously, as wild beasts pursue their prey. But the odd thing was that he never seemed to crave for friendship or intimacy. So far as I know, he had no friends, in the ordinarily accepted sense of the term. He desired only acquaintances and auditors ; and acquaintances and reluctant auditors were all that he had. In the first period of my acquaintance with Peddley I used to wonder what he did when he felt the need of confiding his intimate and private feelings. Later on I came to doubt whether, at ordinary times, he had any private life that needed talking about. Only very rarely and when something catastrophic had explosively shattered the crust of his public existence, did he ever develop a private life. When things were running smoothly in their regular daily grooves, he lived only on the public surface, at the office, at the club, at his own dinner-table, perfectly content so long as there was somebody present to listen to his talk. It mattered not that his auditors might be listening with manifest and extreme reluctance. Like Herbert—and indeed like most bores—John Peddley was more than half unaware of the people upon whom he inflicted himself. He realized that they were there, physically there ; that was all. To their feelings and thoughts he was utterly insensitive. It was this insensitiveness, coupled with his passionate sociability, that gave him his power. He could hunt down his victims and torture them without remorse. The wolf, if he were really sensitive to the feelings of the lamb, might end by turning vegetarian. But he is not sensitive. He is aware only of his own hunger and the deliciousness of mutton. It was the same with John Peddley. Ignorant of the terror which he inspired, of the mental agonies which he inflicted, he could pursue his course relentlessly and with a perfect equanimity.

My first impressions of John Peddley were not unfavourable. True, the halloo with which he greeted Herbert from the quay-side, as we were waiting our turn in the shoving crowd of human sheep to pass down the gangway on to dry land, sounded to me, in my present condition, rather distressingly hearty. And his appearance, when Herbert pointed him out to me, offended me by its robustious healthiness. Nor, when Herbert had introduced us, did I much appreciate the vehemence of his handshake and the loud volubility of his expressions of sympathy. But, on the other hand, he was very kind and efficient. He produced a silver flask from his pocket and made me take a swig of excellent old brandy. Noticing that I was chilled and green with cold, he insisted on my putting on his fur coat. He darted to the custom-house and returned, in an incredibly short space of time, with the official hieroglyph duly chalked upon our suit-cases. A minute later we were sitting in his car, rolling briskly out of Dover along the Canterbury road.

I was feeling, at the time, too ill to think ; and it hardly occurred to me that the situation was, after all, rather odd. Peddley had been waiting on the quay—but not for us ; for we were unexpected. Waiting, then, for whom ? The question did propound itself to me at the time, but uninsistently. There was no room in my mind for anything but the consciousness of sea-sickness. I forgot to wonder, and took my seat in the car, as though it were the most natural thing in the world that we should have been met at the quay by somebody who did not know that we were crossing. And the apparent naturalness of the situation was confirmed for me by the behaviour of my companions. For Peddley had taken it for granted from the first that we should come and stay with him at his country house. And Herbert, for whom one place was always just as good as another, had accepted the invitation at once. I began by protesting ; but feebly, and more out of politeness than in earnest. For it was not essential for me to get back to London that evening ; and the prospect of that dismal journey from Dover, of the cab drive in the chill of the night across London, of a home-coming to fireless and deserted rooms, was very dreadful to me. If I accepted Peddley's invitation, I should find myself in less than half an hour in a warm, comfortable room, at rest and without responsibilities. The temptation to a sea-sick traveller was great ; I succumbed.

' Well,' said Peddley heartily, in his loud, trombone-like voice, ' well, this *is* luck.' He brought down his hand with a tremendous clap on to my knee, as though he were patting

24

a horse. ' The greatest luck ! Think of running into you and Herbert at the gangway ! And carrying you off like this ! Too delightful, too delightful ! '

I was warmed by his gladness ; it seemed so genuine. And genuine it was — the genuine gladness of an ogre who has found a chubby infant straying alone in the woods.

' Extraordinary,' Peddley went on, ' how many acquaintances one meets at Dover quay. I come every day, you know, when I 'm staying in the country ; every day, to meet the afternoon boat. It 's a great resource when one 's feeling dull. All the advantages of a London club in the country. And there 's always time for a good chat before the train starts. That 's what makes me like this district of Kent so much. I 'm trying to persuade my landlord to sell me the house. I 've nearly coaxed him, I think.'

' And then,' said Herbert, who had a way of occasionally breaking his habitual silence with one of those simple and devastatingly judicious reflections which render children so dangerous in polite, adult society, ' and then you 'll find that every one will be travelling by aeroplane. You 'll have to sell the house and move to Croydon, near the aerodrome.'

But Peddley was not the man to be put out by even the most terrible of terrible infants. Wrapped in his insensitiveness, he was not

so much as aware of the infant's terrible-
ness.

'Pooh!' he retorted. 'I don't believe in
aeroplanes. They'll never be safe or cheap
or comfortable enough to compete with the
steamers. Not in our day.' And he embarked
on a long discourse about helicopters and
gyroscopes, air pockets and the cost of petrol.

Meanwhile, I had begun to wonder, in
some alarm, what manner of man this kind,
efficient, hospitable host of mine could be.
A man who, on his own confession, drove
into Dover every afternoon to meet the
packet ; who waylaid sea-sick acquaintances
and had good chats with them while they
waited for the train ; and who so much loved
his afternoon diversions at the quay-side that
he felt moved to refute in serious, technical
argument the prophet of aerial travel. . . .
Decidedly, a strange, a dangerous man.
And his voice, meanwhile, boomed and boomed
in my ears till I felt dizzy with the sound of
it. Too late, it occurred to me that it might
have been better if I had faced that dreary
journey, that chilly drive, that icy and in-
hospitable home-coming to empty rooms.
Too late.

I discovered afterwards that Peddley's
holidays were always spent at railway junctions,
frontier towns and places of international
resort, where he was likely to find a good

supply of victims. For week-ends, Whitsun and Easter, he had his country house near Dover. At Christmas time he always took a week or ten days on the French Riviera. And during the summer he simultaneously satisfied his social passions and his passion for mountain scenery by taking up some strategic position on the Franco-Swiss, Italo-French, or Swiss-Italian frontier, where he could go for walks in the hills and, in the intervals, meet the trans-continental trains. One year he would take his family to Pontarlier ; another to Valorbes ; another to Modane ; another to Brigue ; another to Chiasso. In the course of a few years he had visited all the principal frontier towns in the mountainous parts of central and southern Europe. He knew the best seasons for each. Valorbes, for example, had to be visited early in the season. It was in July and at the beginning of August that the greatest number of English people passed through on their way to Switzerland. When he had seen them on their homeward way at the end of August, Peddley would move on for a fortnight's stay to one of the Italian frontier towns, so as to catch the September tourists on their way to Florence or Venice. His favourite haunt at this season was Modane. There are lots of good walks round Modane ; and the principal trains wait there for two and a half hours.  Rosy with healthful exercise, Peddley would come striding down at the appointed hour to meet the express.  The victim was marked down, caught, and led away to the station buffet.  For the next two hours Peddley indulged in what he called ' a *really* good chat.'

Peddley's circle of acquaintanceship was enormous.  There was his legal practice, to begin with ; that brought him into professional contact with a great variety of people.  Then there were his clubs ; he was a member of three or four, which he frequented assiduously.  And, finally, there was his own constantly hospitable dinner-table ; it is astonishing what even the richest men will put up with for the sake of a good free meal.  He was on talking terms with hundreds, almost thousands, of his fellows.  It was not to be wondered at if he often spied familiar faces in the Modane custom-house.  But there were many days, of course, when nobody of his acquaintance happened to be going South.  On these occasions Peddley would seek out some particularly harassed - looking stranger and offer his assistance.  The kindness, so far as Peddley was concerned, was entirely whole-hearted ; he was not conscious of the wolf concealed beneath his sheep's clothing.  He just felt a desire to be friendly and helpful and, incidentally, chatty.  And helpful he certainly was.  But in the buffet, when the

28

ordeal of the custom-house was over, the
stranger would gradually come to the conclusion, as he listened to Peddley's masterly
exposition of the financial policy of Sweden,
that he would have preferred, on the whole,
to face the rapacious porters and the insolent
douaniers alone and unassisted.

John Peddley had not yet enumerated all
his reasons for supposing that aeroplanes
would never cut out the cross-channel steamers,
when we reached our destination.

'Ah, here we are,' he said, and opened the
door for me to get out. 'But as I was saying,'
he added, turning back to Herbert, 'the great
defect of gyroscopes is their weight and the
excessive rigidity they give to the machine.
Now I grant you, my dear boy . . .'

But I forget what he granted. All I
remember is that he was still granting it when
we entered the drawing-room, where Mrs.
Peddley was sitting with her children.

From the first, I found Grace Peddley
charming. Positively and actively charming.
And yet she was Herbert's own sister and in
many respects very like him. Which only
shows (what, after all, is sufficiently obvious)
that we are prepared to tolerate and even
admire in persons of the opposite sex qualities
which infuriate us when we meet with them
in persons of our own. I found Herbert a
bore because he was mentally blank and

vague, because he was without initiative, because he attached himself and clung. But Grace, whose character was really very similar to Herbert's, charmed me, in spite, or perhaps even because, of these qualities which made me rank her brother among the minor calamities of my existence.

But it is not only the moral and mental qualities of our fellow-beings that inspire our love or hate. I should not, I am sure, have found Herbert so deplorable if he had been smaller and less cumbrous, less clumsy of body. He was altogether too much the lubber fiend for my taste. Physically, Grace displayed little resemblance to her brother. She was tall, it is true, but slim and light of movement. Herbert was thick, shambling and leaden-footed. In a heavy, large-featured way, Herbert was not unhandsome. He had a profile ; his nose and chin were Roman and positively noble. At a distance you might mistake him for some formidable Caesarean man of action. But when you came close enough to see his eyes and read the expression on that large pretentious face, you perceived that, if Roman, he was the dullest and blankest Roman of them all.

Grace was not in the least imposing or classical. You could never, at however great a distance, have mistaken her for the mother of the Gracchi. Her features were small and seemed, somehow, still indefinite, like the features of a child. A lot of dark red-brown hair which, at that epoch, when fashion still permitted women to have hair, she wore looped up in a couple of spirally coiled plaits over either ear, emphasized the pallor of that childish face. A pair of very round, wide-open grey eyes looked out from under the hair with an expression of slightly perplexed ingenuousness. Her face was the face of a rather ugly but very nice little girl. And when she smiled, she was suddenly almost beautiful. Herbert smiled in the same way —a sudden smile, full of kindness and good nature. It was that smile of his that made it impossible, for me at any rate, to treat him with proper ruthlessness. In both of them, brother and sister, it was a singularly dim and helpless goodness that expressed itself in that smile—a gentle, inefficient kindliness that was tinged, in Herbert's case, with a sort of loutish rusticity. He was a bumpkin even in his goodness. Grace's smile was dim, but expressive at the same time of a native refinement which Herbert did not possess. They were brother and sister ; but hers was a soul of better, more aristocratic birth.

It was in her relations with her children that the inefficiency of Grace's benevolence revealed itself most clearly in practice. She loved them, but she didn't know what to do with them or how to treat them. It was lucky for her—and for the children too—that she could afford to keep nurses and governesses. She could never have brought her children up by herself. They would either have died in infancy, or, if they had survived the first two years of unpunctual and hopelessly unhygienic feeding, would have grown up into little savages. As it was, they had been well brought up by professional child-tamers, were healthy and, except towards their mother, beautifully behaved. Their mother, however, they regarded as a being of another species—a lovely and eminently adorable being, but not serious, like nurse or Miss Phillips, not really grown up ; more than half a child, and what wasn't child, mostly fairy. Their mother was the elfin being who permitted or even herself suggested the most fantastic breaches of all the ordinary rules. It was she, for example, who had invented the sport of bathing, in summer-time, under the revolving sprinkler which watered the lawn. It was she who had first suggested that excellent game, so strenuously disapproved of by Miss Phillips, nurse and father, of biting your slice of bread, at dinner-time, into the shape of a flower or a heart, a little bridge, a letter of the alphabet, a triangle, a railway engine. They adored her, but they would not take her seriously, as a person in authority ; it never even occurred to them to obey her.

'You 're a little girl,' I once heard her four-year-old daughter explaining to her. 'You 're a little girl, mummy. Miss Phillips is an old lady.'

Grace turned her wide, perplexed eyes in my direction. 'You see,' she said despairingly, yet with a kind of triumph, as though she were conclusively proving a disputed point, 'you see ! What *can* I do with them ? '

She couldn't do anything. When she was alone with them, the children became like little wild beasts.

'But, children,' she would protest, 'children ! You really mustn't.' But she knew that she might as well have expostulated with a litter of grizzly bears.

Sometimes, when the protest was more than ordinarily loud and despairing, the children would look up from their absorbing mischief and reassuringly smile to her. 'It 's all right, mummy,' they would say. 'It 's quite all right, you know.'

And then, helplessly, their mother would give it up.

In Herbert I found this helpless inefficiency intolerable. But the ineptitude of his sister had a certain style ; even her clumsiness was somehow graceful. For clumsy she was.

When it came to sewing, for example, her fingers were all thumbs. She had quite given up trying to sew when I first knew her. But she still regarded it as part of her maternal duty to knit warm mufflers—she never attempted anything more complicated than a muffler—for the children. She knitted very slowly, painfully concentrating her whole attention on the work in hand until, after a few minutes, exhausted by the mental strain, she was forced, with a great sigh, to give up and take a little rest. A muffler took months to finish. And when it was finished, what an extraordinary object it was ! A sort of woollen fishing-net.

' Not *quite* right, I 'm afraid,' Grace would say, holding it out at arm's length. ' Still,' she added, cocking her head on one side and half closing her eyes, as though she were looking at a *pointilliste* picture, ' it isn't bad, considering.'

Secretly, she was very proud of these mufflers, proud with the pride of a child who has written its first letter or embroidered on canvas its first kettle-holder, with practically no help at all from nurse. It still seemed to her extraordinary that she could do things all by herself, unassisted.

This graceful ineptitude of hers amused and charmed me. True, if I had had to marry it, I might not have found it quite so enchanting, if only for the reason that I should never have been able to afford a sufficiency of servants and child-tamers to counteract its effects on domestic, daily life. Nor, I am afraid, would the absurd charm of her intellectual vagueness have survived a long intimacy. For how vague, how bottomlessly vague she was ! For example, she was quite incapable —and no experience could teach her—of realizing the value of money. At one moment she was lavishly extravagant, would spend pounds as though they were pence. The next, overvaluing her money as wildly as she had undervalued it, she would grudge every penny spent on the first necessities of life. Poor Peddley would sometimes come home from his office to find that there was nothing for dinner but lentils. Another man would have been violently and explosively annoyed ; but Peddley, whose pedagogic passions were more powerful than his anger, only made a reasoned expostulation in the shape of a discourse on the meaning of money and the true nature of wealth, followed by a brief lecture on dietetics and the theory of calories. Grace listened attentively and with humility. But try as she would, she could never remember a word of what he had said ; or rather she remembered, partially, but remembered all wrong. The phrases which Peddley had built up into a rational discourse, Grace rearranged in her mind so as to make complete nonsense. It was the same with what she read. The arguments got turned upside down. The non-essential facts were vividly remembered, the essential forgotten. Dates were utterly meaningless to her. Poor Grace! she was painfully conscious of her inefficiency of mind ; she longed above everything to be learned, authoritative, capable. But though she read a great number of serious books—and read them with genuine pleasure, as well as on principle—she could never contrive to be well read. Inside her head everything got muddled. It was as though her mind were inhabited by some mischievous imp which delighted in taking to pieces the beautifully composed mosaics of learning and genius, and resetting the tesserae (after throwing a good many of them away) in the most fantastic and ludicrous disorder.

The consciousness of these defects made her particularly admire those who were distinguished by the opposite and positive qualities. It was this admiration, I am sure, which made her Peddley's wife. She was very young when he fell in love with her and asked her to marry him—eighteen to his thirty-four or thereabouts—very young and (being fresh from school, with its accompaniment of examination failures and pedagogic reproaches) more than ordinarily sensitive to her own shortcomings and to the merits of those unlike herself. Peddley made his entry into her life. The well-documented accuracy of his knowledge of artificial manures and the Swiss banking system astonished her. True, she did not feel a passionate interest in these subjects ; but for that she blamed herself, not him. He seemed to her the personification of learning and wisdom— omniscient, an encyclopaedia on legs.

It is not uncommon for schoolgirls to fall in love with their aged professors. It is the tribute paid by youth—by flighty, high-spirited, but passionately earnest youth—to venerable mind. Grace was not lucky. The most venerable mind with which, at eighteen, she had yet come into contact was Peddley's. Peddley's ! She admired, she was awed by what seemed to her the towering, Newtonian intellect of the man. And when the Newtonian intellect laid itself at her feet, she felt at first astonished—was it possible that he, Peddley, the omniscient, should abase himself before one who had failed three times, igno-miniously, in the Cambridge Locals ?—then flattered and profoundly grateful. Moreover, Peddley, unlike the proverbial professor, was neither grey-bearded nor decrepit. He was in the prime of life, extremely active, healthy, and energetic ; good-looking, too, in the ruddy, large-chinned style of those Keen Business Men one sees portrayed in advertisements and the illustrations of magazine stories. Quite inexperienced in these matters, she easily persuaded herself that her gratitude and her schoolgirl's excitement were the genuine passion of the novels. She imagined that she was in love with him. And it would have mattered little, in all probability, if she had not. Peddley's tireless courtship would have ended infallibly by forcing her to surrender. There was no strength in Grace ; she could be bullied into anything. In this case, however, only a very little bullying was necessary. At his second proposal, she accepted him. And so, in 1914, a month or two before the outbreak of war, they were married.

A marriage which began with the war might have been expected to be a strange, unusual, catastrophic marriage. But for the Peddleys, as a matter of fact, the war had next to no significance ; it did not touch their life. For the first year John Peddley made Business as Usual his motto. Later, after being rejected for active service on account of his short sight, he enrolled himself as a temporary bureaucrat ; was highly efficient in a number of jobs ; had managed, when the medical boards became stricter, to make himself indispensable, as a sugar rationer ; and ended up with an O.B.E.

Grace, meanwhile, lived quietly at home and gave birth, in three successive years, to three children. They kept her occupied ; the war, for her, was an irrelevance. She witnessed neither its tragedies, nor its feverish and sordid farces. She knew as little of apprehension, suspense, grief, as she knew of the reckless extravagances, the intoxications, the too facile pleasures, the ferocious debaucheries which ran parallel with the agonies, which mingled and alternated with them. Ineffectually, Grace nursed her babies ; she might have been living in the eighteenth century.

At the time I knew her first Grace had been married about six years. Her eldest child was five years old, her youngest about two. Peddley, I judged, was still in love with her—in his own way, that is. The wild passion which had hurried him into a not very reasonable marriage, a passion mainly physical, had subsided. He was no longer mad about Grace ; but he continued to find her eminently desirable. Habit, moreover, had endeared her to him, had made her indispensable ; it had become difficult for him to imagine an existence without her. But for all that, there was no intimacy between them. Possessing, as I have said, no private life of his own, Peddley did not understand the meaning of intimacy. He could give no confidences and therefore asked for none. He did not know what to do with them when they came to him unasked. I do not know if Grace ever tried to confide in him ; if so, she must soon have given it up as a bad job. One might as well have tried to confide into a gramophone ; one might whisper the most secret and sacred thoughts into the trumpet of the machine, but there came back only a loud booming voice that expounded the financial policy of Sweden, food control, or the law relating to insurance companies—it depended which particular record out of the large, but still limited repertory, happened at the moment to be on the turn table. In the spiritual home of the Peddleys there was only a bedroom and a lecture-room—no sentimental boudoir for confidences, no quiet study pleasantly violated from time to time by feminine intrusion. Nothing between the physical intimacies of the bedroom and the impersonal relations of pupil and sonorously braying professor in the reverberant lecture-hall. And then, what lectures !

Grace, who still believed in the intellectual eminence of her husband, continued to blame herself for finding them tedious. But tedious they were to her ; that was a fact she could not deny. Long practice had taught her to cultivate a kind of mental deafness. Peddley's discourses no longer got on her nerves, because she no longer heard them. I have often seen her sitting, her wide eyes turned on Peddley with an expression, apparently, of rapt attention, seeming to drink in every word he uttered. It was so she must have sat in those first months of her marriage, when she really did listen, when she still tried her hardest to be interested and to remember correctly. Only in those days, I fancy, there can never have been quite so perfect a serenity on her face. There must have been little frowns of concentration and agonizingly suppressed yawns. Now there was only an unruffled calm, the calm of complete and absolute abstraction.

I found her out on the very first evening of our acquaintance. John Peddley, who must have been told (I suppose by Herbert) that I was interested, more or less professionally, in music, began, in my honour, a long description of the mechanism of pianolas. I was rather touched by this manifest effort to make me feel spiritually at home, and, though I was dizzied by the sound of his voice, made a great show of being interested in what he was saying. In a pause, while Peddley was helping himself to the vegetables (what a blessing it was to have a moment's respite from that maddening voice !), I turned to Grace and asked her politely, as a new

41

guest should, whether she were as much
interested in pianolas as her husband. She
started, as though I had woken her out of
sleep, turned on me a pair of blank, rather
frightened eyes, blushed scarlet.

'As much interested as John in *what*?'
she asked.

'Pianolas.'

'Oh, pianolas.' And she uttered the word
in a puzzled, bewildered tone which made
it quite clear that she had no idea that pianolas
had been the subject of conversation for at
least the last ten minutes. 'Pianolas?' she
repeated almost incredulously. And she had
seemed so deeply attentive.

I admired her for this power of absenting
herself, for being, spiritually, not there. I
admired, but I also pitied. To have to live
in surroundings from which it was necessary,
in mere self-preservation, to absent oneself—
that was pitiable indeed.

Next morning, assuming an invalid's
privilege, I had breakfast in bed. By the
time I came down from my room, Peddley
and Herbert had set out for a hearty walk.
I found Grace alone, arranging flowers. We
exchanged good-mornings. By the expression
of her face, I could see that she found my
presence rather formidable. A stranger, a
high-brow, a musical critic—what to say to
him? Courageously doing her duty, she

began to talk to me about Bach. Did I like
Bach ? Didn't I think he was the greatest
musician ? I did my best to reply ; but
somehow, at that hour of the morning, there
seemed to be very little to say about Bach.
The conversation began to droop.

'And the *Well-Tempered Clavichord*,' she
went on desperately. 'What lovely things
in that ! '

'And so useful for torturing children who
learn the piano,' I replied, as desperately.
Facetiousness, the last resort.

But my words had touched a chord in
Grace's mind. 'Torture,' she said. 'That's
the word. I remember when I was at
school . . .'

And there we were, happily launched at last
upon an interesting, because a personal, subject.

Grace was as fond of her dear old school
as Herbert was of his. But, with the rest
of her sex, she had a better excuse for her
fondness. For many women, the years spent
in that uncomplicated, companionable, exciting, purely feminine world, which is the
world of school, are the happiest of their
lives. Grace was one of them. She adored
her school ; she looked back on her schooldays
as on a golden age. True, there had been
Cambridge Locals and censorious mistresses ;
but on the other hand, there had been no
Peddley, no annual child-bearing, no domestic

responsibilities, no social duties, no money
to be too lavish or too stingy with, no servants.
She talked with enthusiasm, and I listened
with pleasure.

An hour and a half later, when the bores
came back, red-faced and ravenous, from
their walk, we were sorry to be interrupted.
I had learned a great many facts about Grace's
girlhood. I knew that she had had an unhappy passion for the younger of the visiting
music mistresses ; that one of her friends
had received a love-letter from a boy of
fifteen, beginning : 'I saw a photograph of
you in the *Sketch*, walking in the Park with
your mother. Can I ever forget it ?' I
knew that she had had mumps for five weeks,
that she had climbed on the roof by moonlight
in pyjamas, that she was no good at hockey.

From time to time most of us feel a need,
often urgent and imperious, to talk about ourselves. We desire to assert our personalities,
to insist on a fact which the world about us
seems in danger of forgetting—the fact that
we exist, that we are we. In some people
the desire is so chronic and so strong, that
they can never stop talking about themselves.
Rather than be silent, they will pour out the
most humiliating and discreditable confidences.
Grace was afflicted by no such perverse and
extravagant longings ; there was nothing of
the exhibitionist in her. But she did like,

every now and then, to have a good talk about her soul, her past history, her future. She liked to talk, and she too rarely had an opportunity. In me she found a sympathetic listener and commentator. By the end of the morning she was regarding me as an old friend. And I, for my part, had found her charming. So charming, indeed, that for Grace's sake I was prepared to put up even with John Peddley's exposition of the law regarding insurance companies.

Within a few weeks of our first introduction we were finding it the most natural thing in the world that we should be constantly meeting. We talked a great deal, on these occasions, about ourselves, about Life and about Love—subjects which can be discussed with the fullest pleasure and profit only between persons of opposite sexes. On none of these three topics, it must be admitted, did Grace have very much of significance to say. She had lived very little and loved not at all ; it was impossible, therefore, that she should know herself. But it was precisely this ignorance and her ingenuous, confident expression of it that charmed me.

' I feel I 'm already old,' she complained to me. ' Old and finished. Like those funny straw hats and leg-of-mutton sleeves in the bound volumes of the *Illustrated London News*,' she added, trying to make her meaning clearer for me.

I laughed at her. 'You're absurdly young,' I said, 'and you haven't begun.'

She shook her head and sighed.

When we talked about love, she professed a sad, middle-aged scepticism.

'People make a most ridiculous fuss about it.'

'Rightly.'

'But it's not worth making a fuss about,' she insisted. 'Not in reality. Not outside of books.'

'Isn't it?' I said. 'You'll think differently,' I told her, 'when you've waited two or three hours for somebody who hasn't turned up, when you can't sleep for wondering where somebody's been and with whom, and you want to cry—yes, you do cry—and you feel as though you were just going to have influenza.'

'Ah, but that isn't love,' Grace retorted sententiously, in the tone of one who has some private and certain source of information.

'What is it, then?'

'It's . . .' Grace hesitated and suddenly blushed, 'it's . . . well, it's physical.'

I could not help laughing, uproariously.

Grace was vexed. 'Well, isn't it true?' she insisted obstinately.

'Perfectly,' I had to admit. 'But why isn't that love?' I added, hoping to elicit Grace's views on the subject.

She let me have them. They were positively Dantesque. I can only suppose that Peddley's ardours had left her cold, disgusted even.

But Life and Love were not our only topics. Grace's ignorance and my own native reticence made it impossible for us to discuss these themes with any profit for very long at a stretch. In the intervals, like John Peddley, I played the pedagogic part. Through casual remarks of mine, Grace suddenly became aware of things whose very existence had previously been unknown to her— things like contemporary painting and literature, young music, new theories of art. It was a revelation. All her efforts, it seemed to her, all her strivings towards culture had been wasted. She had been laboriously trying to scale the wrong mountain, to force her way into the wrong sanctuary. At the top, if she had ever reached it, within the holy of holies, she would have found — what? a grotesque and moth-eaten collection of those funny little straw hats and leg-of-mutton sleeves from the bound volumes of the *Illustrated London News*. It was dreadful, it was humiliating. But now she had caught a glimpse of another sanctuary, upholstered by Martine, enriched by the offerings of the Poirets and Lanvins of the spirit ; a modish, modern sanctuary ; a fashionable Olympus. She was eager to climb, to enter.

Acting the part of those decayed gentle-
women who, for a consideration, introduce
*parvenus* into good society, I made Grace
acquainted with all that was smartest and
latest in the world of the spirit. I gave her
lessons in intellectual etiquette, warned her
against aesthetic *gaffes*. She listened attentively, and was soon tolerably at home in the
unfamiliar world—knew what to say when
confronted by a Dada poem, a picture by
Picasso, a Schoenberg quartet, an Archipenko
sculpture.

I was working, at that period, as a musical
critic, and two or three times a week I used
to take Grace with me to my concerts. It
did not take me long to discover that she had
very little feeling for music and no analytical
understanding of it. But she professed,
hypocritically, to adore it. And as it bored
me most excruciatingly to have to go by
myself to listen to second-rate pianists playing
the same old morsels of Liszt and Chopin,
second-rate contraltos fruitily hooting Schubert
and Brahms, second-rate fiddlers scraping
away at Tartini and Wieniawski, I pretended
to believe in Grace's enthusiasm for the
musical art and took her with me to all the
most painful recitals. If the hall were empty
—which, to the eternal credit of the music-
loving public, it generally was—one could
get a seat at the back, far away from the other

sparsely sprinkled auditors, and talk very pleasantly through the whole performance.

At first, Grace was terribly shocked when, after listening judicially to the first three bars of *Du bist wie eine Blume* or the *Trillo del Diavolo*, I opened a conversation. She herself had a very perfect concert-goer's technique, and listened with the same expression of melancholy devotion, as though she were in church, to every item on the programme. My whispered chatter seemed to her sacrilegious. It was only when I assured her, professionally and *ex cathedra*, that the stuff wasn't worth listening to, that she would consent, albeit with considerable misgivings in the early days of our concert-going, to take her part in the conversation. In a little while, however, she grew accustomed to the outrage ; so much so, that when the music or the performance happened to be good (a little detail which Grace was not sufficiently musical to notice) it was I who had to play the verger's part and hush her sacrilegious chatter in a place suddenly made holy. She learned in the end to take her cue from me —to look devout when I looked devout, to chatter when I chattered.

Once, rather maliciously, I put on my raptest expression while some maudlin incompetent was pounding out Rachmaninoff. After a quick glance at me through the tail of her eye, Grace also passed into ecstasy, gazing at the pianist as St. Theresa might have gazed at the uplifted Host. When the ordeal was over, she turned on me a pair of bright, shining eyes.

'Wasn't that splendid?' she said. And such is the power of self-suggestion, that she had genuinely enjoyed it.

'I thought it the most revolting performance I ever listened to,' was my answer.

Poor Grace turned fiery red, the tears came into her eyes; to hide them from me, she averted her face. 'I thought it very good,' she insisted, heroically. 'But of course I'm no judge.'

'Oh, of course it wasn't as bad as all that,' I made haste to assure her. 'One exaggerates, you know.' The sight of her unhappy face had made me feel profoundly penitent. I had meant only to make mild fun of her, and I had managed somehow to hurt her, cruelly. I wished to goodness that I had never played the stupid trick. It was a long time before she completely forgave me.

Later, when I knew her better, I came to understand why it was that she had taken my little clownery so hardly. Rudely and suddenly, my joke had shattered one of those delightful pictures of herself which Grace was for ever fancifully creating and trying to live up to. What had been a joke for me had been, for her, a kind of murder.

Grace was a born visualizer. I discovered, for example, that she had what Galton calls a 'number form.' When she had to do any sort of arithmetical calculation, she saw the figures arranged in space before her eyes. Each number had its own peculiar colour and its own position in the form. After a hundred the figures became dim ; that was why she always found it so difficult to work in large numbers. The difference between three thousand, thirty thousand, and three hundred thousand was never immediately apparent to her, because in the case of these large numbers she could *see* nothing ; they floated indistinctly on the blurred fringes of her number form. A million, however, she saw quite clearly ; its place was high up, to the left, above her head, and it consisted of a huge pile of those envelopes they have at banks for putting money in—thousands and thousands of them, each marked with the word MILLION in large black letters. All her mental processes were a succession of visual images ; and these mental pictures were so vivid as to rival in brightness and definition the images she received through her eyes. What she could not visualize, she could not think about.

I am myself a very poor visualizer. I should find it very difficult, for example, to describe from memory the furniture in my room. I know that there are so many chairs, so many tables, doors, bookshelves, and so on ; but I have no clear mental vision of them. When I do mental arithmetic, I see no coloured numbers. The word Africa does not call up in my mind, as Grace assured me once that it always did in hers, a vision of sand with palm trees and lions. When I make plans for the future, I do not see myself, as though on the stage, playing a part in imaginary dramas. I think without pictures, abstractly and in the void. That is why I cannot pretend to write with complete understanding of the workings of Grace's mind. The congenitally deaf are not the best judges of music. I can only guess, only imaginatively reconstruct.

From what I gathered in conversation with her, I imagine that Grace was in the habit of vividly ' seeing herself ' in every kind of situation. Some of these situations had no relation to her actual life, were the purely fantastic and hypothetical situations of day-dreams. Others were real, or at any rate potentially real, situations. Living her life, she saw herself living it, acting in the scenes of the flat quotidian drama a very decided and definite part. Thus, when she went for a walk in the country, she saw herself walking— a female mountaineer for tireless strength and energy. When she accompanied Peddley on his annual expeditions to the Riviera, she saw herself as she climbed into the *wagon lit*, or swam along the Promenade des Anglais, as an immensely rich and haughty milady, envied by the *canaille*, remote and star-like above them. On certain socially important occasions at home, a similar character made its appearance. I saw the milady once or twice during the first months of our acquaintance-ship. Later on the milady turned into a very Parisian, very twentieth-cum-eighteenth-century *grande dame*. But of that in its placc.

Grace was much assisted in these visualizations of herself by her clothes. In the costume which she donned for a two-mile walk in Kent she might have crossed the Andes. And in all her garments, for every occasion, one noticed the same dramatic appropriateness. It was a pity that she did not know how to change her features with her clothes. Her face, whether she lolled along the sea-fronts of the Riviera or addressed herself, in brogues, short skirts, and sweaters to the ascent of some Kentish hillock, was always the same—the face of a rather ugly but very nice little girl ; a face that opened on to the world through large, perplexed eyes, and that became, from time to time, suddenly and briefly beautiful with a dim benevolence when she smiled.

Grace's visions of herself were not merely momentary and occasional. There was generally one predominating character in which she saw herself over considerable periods

of time. During the first four years of her
marriage, for example, she had seen herself
predominantly as the housewife and mother.
But her manifest incapacity to act either of
these parts successfully had gradually chilled
her enthusiasm for them. She wanted to run
the house, she saw herself tinkling about with
keys, giving orders to the maids ; but, in
practice, whenever she interfered with the
rule of her masterful old cook, everything
went wrong. She loved her children, she
pictured them growing up, healthy and good,
under her influence ; but they were always
sick when she fed them, they behaved like
beasts when she tried to make them obey.
To one who tried to see herself as the complete,
the almost German matron, it was not encouraging. By the time her last child was
born, she had practically abandoned the
attempt. From the first, the baby had been
handed over, body and soul, to the nurses.
And except when she was seized with a
financial panic and forbade the ordering of
anything but lentils, she let the old cook have
her way.

When I first met her, Grace was not seeing
herself continuously in any one predominating
rôle. Punctured by sharp experience, the
matron had flattened out and collapsed ; and
the matron had had, so far, no successor.
Left without an imaginary character to live

up to, Grace had relapsed into that dim char-
acterlessness which in her, as in Herbert,
seemed to be the natural state.  She still saw
herself vividly enough in the separate, occasional incidents of her life—as the mountain
climber, as the rich and haughty milady.
But she saw no central and permanent figure
in whose life these incidents of mountaineering
and opulently visiting the Riviera occurred.
She was a succession of points, so to speak ;
not a line.

Her friendship with me was responsible for
the emergence into her consciousness of a new
permanent image of herself.  She discovered
in my company a new rôle, not so important,
indeed, not so rich in potentialities as that of
the matron, but still a leading lady's part.
She had been so long without a character
that she eagerly embraced the opportunity of
acquiring one, however incongruous.  And
incongruous it was, this new character ; odd
and eminently unsuitable.  Grace had come
to see herself as a musical critic.

It was our concert-going—our professional
concert-going—that had done it.  If I had
happened not to be a journalist, if we had paid
for admission instead of coming in free on my
complimentary tickets, it would never have
occurred to her to see herself as a critic.
Simple mortals, accustomed to pay for their
pleasures, are always impressed by the sight

of a free ticket. The critic's *jus primae noctis* seems to them an enviable thing. Sharing the marvellous privilege, Grace came to feel that she must also share the judicial duties of a critic. She saw herself distributing praise and blame—a rapturous listener when the performance was worth listening to, a contemptuous chatterer when it wasn't. Identifying herself with me—not the real but an ideal exalted me—she pictured herself as the final arbiter of musical reputations. My malicious little practical joke had thrown down this delightful image of herself. The critic had suddenly been murdered.

At the time I did not understand why poor Grace should have been so deeply hurt. It was only in the light of my later knowledge that I realized what must have been her feelings. It was only later, too, that I came to understand the significance of that curious little pantomime which she used regularly to perform as we entered a concert hall. That languid gait with which she strolled across the vestibule, dragging her feet with a kind of reluctance, as though she were on boring business ; that sigh, that drooping of the eyelids as she stood, patiently, while the attendant looked at my tickets ; that air, when we were in the concert-room, of being perfectly at home, of owning the place (she used, I remember, to put her feet up on the seat in front) ; and that smile of overacted contempt, that wearily amused smile with which she used (once she had got over the idea that she was committing a sacrilege) to respond, during a bad performance, to my whispered chatter—these were the gait, the bored patience, the possessive at-homeness, the contempt of a hardened critic.

And what a quantity of music she bought at this time and never played ! How many volumes of musical criticism and biography she took out of the library ! And the grave pronouncements she used to make across the dinner-table ! ' Beethoven was the greatest of them all ' ; and so on in the same style. I understood it all afterwards. And the better I understood, the more I regretted my cruel little joke. As the critic, she had been so happy. My joke destroyed that happiness. She became diffident and self-conscious, got actor's fright ; and though I never repeated the jest, though I always encouraged her, after that, to believe in her musicianship, she could never whole-heartedly see herself in the part again.

But what a poor part, at the best of times, the critic's was ! It was too dry, too intellectual and impersonal to be really satisfying. That it lay within my power to provide her with a much better rôle—the guilty wife's—I do not and did not at the time much doubt. True, when I knew her first, Grace was a

perfectly virtuous young woman. But her
virtue was founded on no solid principle—
on a profound love for her husband, for
example ; or on strong religious prejudices.
It was not a virtue that in any way involved
her intimate being. If she happened to be
virtuous, it was more by accident than on
principle or from psychological necessity.
She had not yet had any occasion for not being
virtuous, that was all. She could have been
bullied or cajoled into infidelity as she had
been bullied and cajoled by Peddley into
marriage. Grace floated vaguely on the
surface of life without compass or destination ;
one had only to persuade her that adultery
was Eldorado, and she would have shaped her
course forthwith towards that magical shore.
It was just a question of putting the case
sufficiently speciously. She still retained, at
this time, the prejudices of her excellent upper
middle-class upbringing ; but they were not
very deeply rooted. Nothing in Grace was
so deeply rooted that it could not quite easily
be eradicated.

I realized these facts at the time. But I
did not try to take advantage of them. The
truth is that, though I liked Grace very much,
I was never urgently in love with her. True,
one can very agreeably and effectively act the
part of the ' lover,' in the restricted and technical sense of that term, without being wildly

in love.  And if both parties could always
guarantee to keep their emotions in a state of
equilibrium, these little sentimental sensualities would doubtless be most exquisitely
diverting.  But the equilibrium can never be
guaranteed.  The balanced hearts begin
sooner or later, almost inevitably, to tilt
towards love or hatred.  In the end, one of
the sentimental sensualities turns into a
passion—whether of longing or disgust it
matters not—and then, farewell to all hope of
tranquillity.  I should be chary of saying so
in Kingham's presence ; but the fact remains
that I like tranquillity.  For me, the love-game,
without love, is not worth the candle.  Even
as a mere hedonist I should have refrained.
And I had other scruples—scruples which an
overmastering passion might have overridden,
but which were sufficient to keep a mere mild
sensuality in check.  I was never Grace's
lover ; neither genuinely, by right of passion,
nor technically by the accident of physical
possession.  Never her lover.  An ironic fate
had reserved for me a less glorious part—the
part, not of the lover, but of the introducer of
lovers.  All unintentionally, I was to play
benevolent Uncle Pandarus to Grace's Cres-
sida.  And there were two Troiluses.

The first of them was no less—or shouldn't
I rather say ' no more ' ? for how absurdly his
reputation was  exaggerated !—than Clegg,

*the* Clegg, Rodney Clegg, the painter. I have known Clegg for years and liked him, in a way—liked him rather as one likes Grock, or Little Tich, or the Fratellini : as a comic spectacle. This is not the best way of liking people, I know. But with Rodney it was the only way. You had either to like him as a purveyor of amusement, or dislike him as a human being. That, at any rate, was always my experience. I have tried hard to get to know and like him intimately—off the stage, so to speak. But it was never any good. In the end, I gave up the attempt once and for all, took to regarding him quite frankly as a music-hall comedian, and was able, in consequence, thoroughly to enjoy his company. Whenever I feel like a tired business man, I go to see Rodney Clegg.

Perhaps, as a lover, Rodney was somehow different from his ordinary self. Perhaps he dropped his vanity and his worldliness. Perhaps he became unexpectedly humble and unselfish, forgot his snobbery, craved no longer for cheap successes and, for love, thought the world well lost. Perhaps. Or more probably, I am afraid, he remained very much as he always was, and only in Grace's eyes seemed different from the Rodney whose chatter and little antics diverted the tired business man in me. Was hers the correct vision of him, or was mine ? Neither, I take it.

It must have been in the spring of 1921 that I first took Grace to Rodney's studio. For her, the visit was an event ; she was about to see, for the first time in her life, a famous man. Particularly famous at the moment, it happened ; for Rodney was very much in the papers that season. There had been a fuss about his latest exhibition. The critics, with a fine contemptuous inaccuracy, had branded his pictures as post-impressionistic, cubistic, futuristic ; they threw any brick-bat that came to hand. And the pictures had been found improper as well as disturbingly ' modern.' Professional moralists had been sent by the Sunday papers to look at them ; they came back boiling with professional indignation. Rodney was delighted, of course. This was fame—and a fame, moreover, that was perfectly compatible with prosperity. The outcry of the professional moralists did not interfere with his sales. He was doing a very good business.

Rodney's conversion to ' modern art,' instead of ruining him, had been the source of increased profit and an enhanced notoriety. With his unfailing, intuitive knowledge of what the public wanted, he had devised a formula which combined modernity with the more appealing graces of literature and pornography. Nothing, for example, could have been less academic than his nudes. They were monstrously elongated ; the paint was laid on quite flatly ; there was no modelling, no realistic light and shade ; the human form was reduced to a paper silhouette. The eyes were round black boot-buttons, the nipples magenta berries, the lips vermilion hearts ; the hair was represented by a collection of crinkly black lines. The exasperated critics of the older school protested that a child of ten could have painted them. But the child of ten who could have painted such pictures must have been an exceedingly perverse child. In comparison, Freud's Little Hans would have been an angel of purity. For Rodney's nudes, however unrealistic, were luscious and voluptuous, were even positively indecent. What had distressed the public in the work of the French post-impressionists was not so much the distortion and the absence of realism as the repellant austerity, the intellectual asceticism, which rejected the appeal both of sex and of the anecdote. Rodney had supplied the deficiencies. For these engagingly luscious nudities of his were never repre- sented in the void, so to speak, but in all sorts of curious and amusing situations—taking tickets at railway stations, or riding bicycles, or sitting at cafés with negro jazz-bands in the background, drinking *crème de menthe*. All the people who felt that they ought to be in the movement, that it was a disgrace not to like modern art, discovered in Rodney Clegg, to their enormous delight, a modern artist whom they could really and honestly admire. His pictures sold like hot cakes.

The conversion to modernism marked the real beginning of Rodney's success. Not that he had been unknown or painfully poor before his conversion. A man with Rodney's social talents, with Rodney's instinct for popularity, could never have known real obscurity or poverty. But all things are relative ; before his conversion, Rodney had been obscurer and poorer than he deserved to be. He knew no duchesses, no millionairesses, then ; he had no deposit at the bank—only a current account that swelled and ebbed capriciously, like a mountain stream. His conversion changed all that.

When Grace and I paid our first visit, he was already on the upward path.

' I hope he isn't very formidable,' Grace said to me, as we were making our way to Hampstead to see him. She was always rather frightened by the prospect of meeting new people.

I laughed. ' It depends what you 're afraid of,' I said. ' Of being treated with high-brow haughtiness, or losing your virtue. I never heard of any woman who found him formidable in the first respect.'

' Oh, that 's all right, then,' said Grace, looking relieved.

Certainly, there was nothing very formidable in Rodney's appearance. At the age of thirty-five he had preserved (and he also cultivated with artful care) the appearance of a good-looking boy. He was small and neatly made, slim, and very agile in his movements. Under a mass of curly brown hair, which was always in a state of picturesque and studied untidiness, his face was like the face of a lively and impertinent cherub. Smooth, rounded, almost unlined, it still preserved its boyish contours. (There were always pots and pots of beauty cream on his dressing-table.) His eyes were blue, bright and expressive. He had good teeth, and when he smiled two dimples appeared in his cheeks.

He opened the studio door himself. Dressed in his butcher's blue overalls, he looked charming. One's instinct was to pat the curly head and say : ' Isn't he too sweet ! Dressed up like that, pretending to be a workman ! ' Even I felt moved to make some such gesture. To a woman, a potential mother of chubby children, the temptation must have been almost irresistible.

Rodney was very cordial. ' Dear old Dick ! ' he said, and patted me on the shoulder. I had not seen him for some months ; he had spent the winter abroad. ' What a delight to see you ! ' I believe he genuinely liked me.

I introduced him to Grace. He kissed her

hand. ' Too charming of you to have come.
And what an enchanting ring ! ' he added,
looking down again at her hand, which he
still held in his own. ' Do, please, let me
look at it.'

Grace smiled and blushed with pleasure as
she gave it him. ' I got it in Florence,' she
said. ' I 'm so glad you like it.'

It was certainly a charming piece of old
Italian jewellery. Sadly I reflected that I had
known Grace intimately for more than six
months and never so much as noticed the ring,
far less made any comment on it. No wonder
that I had been generally unlucky in love.

We found the studio littered with specimens
of Rodney's latest artistic invention. Naked
ladies in brown boots leading borzoi dogs ;
tenderly embracing one another in the middle
of a still-life of bottles, guitars and newspapers (the old familiar modern still-life
rendered acceptable to the great public and
richly saleable by the introduction of the
equivocal nudes) ; more naked ladies riding
on bicycles (Rodney's favourite subject, his
patent, so to say) ; playing the concertina ;
catching yellow butterflies in large green nets.
Rodney brought them out one by one. From
her arm-chair in front of the easel, Grace
looked at them ; her face wore that rapt
religious expression which I had so often
noticed in the concert-room.

' Lovely,' she murmured, as canvas succeeded canvas, ' too lovely.'

Looking at the pictures, I reflected with some amusement that, a year before, Rodney had been painting melodramatic crucifixions in the style of Tiepolo. At that time he had been an ardent Christian.

' Art can't live without religion,' he used to say then. ' We must get back to religion.'

And with his customary facility Rodney had got back to it. Oh, those pictures ! They were really shocking in their accomplished insincerity. So emotional, so dramatic, and yet so utterly false and empty. The subjects, you felt, had been apprehended as a cinema producer might apprehend them, in terms of ' effectiveness.' There were always great darknesses and tender serene lights, touches of vivid colour and portentous silhouettes. Very ' stark,' was what Rodney's admirers used to call those pictures, I remember. They were too stark by half for my taste.

Rodney set up another canvas on the easel.

' I call this " The Bicycle made for Two," ' he said.

It represented a negress and a blonde with a Chinese white skin, riding on a tandem bicycle against a background of gigantic pink and yellow roses. In the foreground, on the right, stood a plate of fruit, tilted forward towards the spectator, in the characteristic ' modern '

style.  A greyhound trotted along beside the
bicycle.

'Really too . . .' began Grace ecstatically.
But finding no synonym for 'lovely,' the
epithet which she had applied to all the other
pictures, she got no further, but made one of
those non-committal laudatory noises, which
are so much more satisfactory than articulate
speech, when you don't know what to say to
an artist about his works.  She looked up at
me.  'Isn't it really . . . ?' she asked.

'Yes, absolutely . . .'  I nodded my affir-
mation.  Then, rather maliciously, 'Tell me,
Rodney,' I said, 'do you still paint religious
pictures?  I remember a most grandiose
Descent from the Cross you were busy on
not so long ago.'

But my malice was disappointed.  Rodney
was not in the least embarrassed by this
reminder of the skeleton in his cupboard.
He laughed.

'Oh, *that*,' he said.  'I painted it over.
Nobody would buy.  One cannot serve God
and Mammon.'  And he laughed again,
heartily, at his own witticism.

It went into his repertory at once, that little
joke.  He took to introducing the subject of
his religious paintings himself, in order to
have an opportunity of bringing out the
phrase, with a comical parody of clerical
unction, at the end of his story.  In the course

of the next few weeks I heard him repeat it, in
different assemblages, three or four times.

'God and Mammon,' he chuckled again.
'Can't be combined.'

'Only goddesses and Mammon,' I suggested, nodding in the direction of his picture.

Later, I had the honour of hearing my words
incorporated into Rodney's performance. He
had a wonderfully retentive memory.

'Precisely,' he said. 'Goddesses, I 'm
happy to say, of a more popular religion.
Are you a believer, Mrs. Peddley ? ' He
smiled at her, raising his eyebrows. ' I am—
fervently. I 'm *croyant* and ' (he emphasized
the ' and ' with arch significance) ' *pratiquant*.'

Grace laughed rather nervously, not knowing
what to answer. ' Well, I suppose we all are,'
she said. She was not accustomed to this
sort of gallantry.

Rodney smiled at her more impertinently
than ever. ' How happy I should be,' he
said, ' if I could make a convert of you ! '

Grace repeated her nervous laugh and, to
change the subject, began to talk about the
pictures.

We sat there for some time, talking, drinking tea, smoking cigarettes. I looked at my
watch ; it was half-past six. I knew that
Grace had a dinner-party that evening.

'We shall have to go,' I said to her.
'You 'll be late for your dinner.'

'Good heavens!' cried Grace, when she heard what the time was. She jumped up. 'I must fly. Old Lady Wackerbath—imagine if I kept her waiting!' She laughed, but breathlessly; and she had gone quite pale with anticipatory fright.

'Stay, do stay,' implored Rodney. 'Keep her waiting.'

'I daren't.'

'But, my dear lady, you're young,' he insisted; 'you have the right—I'd say the duty, if the word weren't so coarse and masculine—to be unpunctual. At your age you must do what you like. You see, I'm assuming that you like being here,' he added parenthetically.

She returned his smile. 'Of course.'

'Well then, stay; do what you like; follow your caprices. After all, that's what you're there for.' Rodney was very strong on the Eternal Feminine.'

Grace shook her head. 'Good-bye. I've loved it so much.'

Rodney sighed, looked sad and slowly shook his head. 'If you'd loved it as much as all that,' he said, 'as much as I've loved it, you wouldn't be saying good-bye. But if you must. . . .' He smiled seductively; the teeth flashed, the dimples punctually appeared. He took her hand, bent over it and tenderly kissed it. 'You must come again,' he added. 'Soon.

And,' turning to me with a laugh, and patting my shoulder, ' without old Dick.'

' He 's frightfully amusing, isn't he ? ' Grace said to me a minute later when we had left the studio.

' Frightfully,' I agreed, laying a certain emphasis on the adverb.

' And really,' she continued, ' most awfully nice, I thought.'

I made no comment.

' And a wonderful painter,' she added.

All at once I felt that I detested Rodney Clegg. I thought of my own sterling qualities of mind and heart, and it seemed to me outrageous, it seemed to me scandalous and intolerable that people, that is to say women in general, and Grace in particular, should be impressed and taken in and charmed by this little middle-aged charlatan with the pretty boy's face and the horribly knowing, smart, impertinent manner. It seemed to me a disgrace. I was on the point of giving vent to my indignation ; but it occurred to me, luckily, just in time that I should only be quite superfluously making a fool of myself if I did. Nothing is more ridiculous than a scene of jealousy, particularly when the scene is made by somebody who has no right to make it and on no grounds whatever. I held my tongue. My indignation against Rodney died down ; I was able to laugh at myself. But

driving southward through the slums of
Camden Town, I looked attentively at Grace
and found her more than ordinarily charming,
desirable even. I would have liked to tell her
so and, telling, kiss her. But I lacked the
necessary impudence ; I felt diffident of my
capacity to carry the amorous undertaking
through to a successful issue. I said nothing,
risked no gesture. But I decided, when the
time should come for us to part, that I would
kiss her hand. It was a thing I had never
done before. At the last moment, however, it
occurred to me that she might imagine that,
in kissing her hand, I was only stupidly
imitating Rodney Clegg. I was afraid she
might think that his example had emboldened
me. We parted on the customary handshake.

Four or five weeks after our visit to Rodney's
studio, I went abroad for a six months' stay in
France and Germany. In the interval, Grace
and Rodney had met twice, the first time in
my flat, for tea, the second at her house, where
she had asked us both to lunch. Rodney was
brilliant on both occasions. A little too
brilliant indeed—like a smile of false teeth, I
thought. But Grace was dazzled. She had
never met any one like this before. Her
admiration delighted Rodney.

' Intelligent woman,' was his comment, as
we left her house together after lunch.

A few days later I set out for Paris.

'You must promise to write,' said Grace in a voice full of sentiment when I came to say good-bye.

I promised, and made her promise too. I did not know exactly why we should write to one another or what we should write about ; but it seemed, none the less, important that we should write. Letter-writing has acquired a curious sentimental prestige which exalts it, in the realm of friendship, above mere conversation ; perhaps because we are less shy at long range than face to face, because we dare to say more in written than in spoken words.

It was Grace who first kept her promise.

'MY DEAR DICK,' she wrote. 'Do you remember what you said about Mozart ? That his music seems so gay on the surface— so gay and careless ; but underneath it is sad and melancholy, almost despairing. I think life is like that, really. Everything goes with such a bustle ; but what's it all for ? And how sad, how sad it is ! Now you mustn't flatter yourself by imagining that I feel like this just because you happen to have gone away—though as a matter of fact I *am* sorry you aren't here to talk about music and people and life and so forth. No, don't flatter yourself ; because I've really felt like this for years, almost for ever. It's, so to speak, the bass of my music, this feeling ; it throbs along all the time, regardless of what may be happening in the treble. Jigs, minuets, mazurkas, Blue Danube waltzes ; but the bass remains the same. This isn't very good counterpoint, I know ; but you see what I mean ? The children have just left me, yelling. Phyllis has just smashed that hideous Copenhagen rabbit Aunt Eleanor gave me for Christmas. I'm delighted, of course ; but I mayn't say so. And in any case, why must they always act such knockabouts ? Sad, sad. And Lecky's *History of European Morals*, that's sadder still. It's a book I can never find my place in. Page 100 seems exactly the same as page 200. No clue. So that—you know how conscientious I am—I always have to begin again at the beginning. It's very discouraging. I haven't the spirit to begin again, yet again, this evening. I write to you instead. But in a moment I must go and dress for dinner. John's partner is coming ; surely no man has a right to be so bald. And Sir Walter Magellan, who is something at the Board of Trade and makes jokes; with Lady M——, who's *so* affectionate. She has a way of kissing me, suddenly and intently, like a snake striking. And she spits when she talks. Then there's Molly Bone, who's so nice ; but why can't she get married ? And the Robsons, about whom there's nothing to say. Nothing whatever. Nothing, nothing,

nothing. That's how I feel about it all. I shall put on my old black frock and wear no jewels. Good-bye.                GRACE.'

Reading this letter, I regretted more than ever my lack of impudence and enterprise in the taxi, that day we had driven down from Rodney's studio. It seemed to me, now, that the impudence would not have been resented.

I returned a letter of consolation ; wrote again a week later ; again ten days after that ; and again, furiously, after another fortnight. A letter at last came back. It smelt of sandal-wood and the stationery was pale yellow. In the past, Grace's correspondence had always been odourless and white. I looked and sniffed with a certain suspicion ; then un-folded and read.

' I am surprised, my good Dick,' the letter began, ' that you don't know us better. Haven't you yet learned that we women don't like the sound of the words Must and Ought ? We can't abide to have our sense of duty appealed to. That was why I never answered any of your impertinent letters. They were too full of " you must write, and " you pro-mised." What do I care what I promised ? That was long ago. I am a different being now. I have been thousands of different beings since then—re-born with each caprice. Now, at last, I choose, out of pure grace and kindness, to relent. Here's a letter. But

beware of trying to bully me again ; don't
ever attempt to blackmail my conscience.    I
may be crueller next time.    This is a warning.

'Were you trying, with your descriptions of
diversions and entertainments, to make me
envious of your Paris ?  If so, you haven't
succeeded.    We have our pleasures here too
—even in London.    For example, the most
exquisite masked ball a few days since.    Like
Longhi's Venice or Watteau's Cythera—and
at moments, let me add, towards the end of the
evening, almost like Casanova's Venice, almost
like the gallant, *grivois* Arcadia of Boucher.
But hush !    It was in Chelsea ;  I 'll tell you
no more.    You might come bursting in on
the next dance, pulling a long face because the
band wasn't playing Bach and the dancers
weren't talking about the " Critique of Pure
Reason."    For the fact is, my poor Dick,
you 're too solemn and serious in your pleasures.
I shall really have to take you in hand, when
you come back.    You must be taught to be
a little lighter and more fantastic.    For the
truth about you is that you 're absurdly
Victorian.    You 're still at the Life-is-real-life-
is-earnest,    Low - living - and - high - thinking
stage.    You lack the courage of your instincts.
I want to see you more frivolous and sociable,
yes, and more gluttonous and lecherous, my
good Dick.    If I were as free as you are, oh,
what an Epicurean I 'd be !    Repent of your

75

ways, Dick, before it 's too late and you 're irrecoverably middle-aged. No more. I am being called away on urgent pleasure. GRACE.'

I read through this extraordinary epistle several times. If the untidy, illegible writing had not been so certainly Grace's, I should have doubted her authorship of the letter. That sham *dix-huitième* language, those neo-rococo sentiments—these were not hers. I had never heard her use the words ' caprice ' or ' pleasure ' ; she had never generalized in that dreadfully facile way about ' we women.' What, then, had come over the woman since last she wrote ? I put the two letters together. What could have happened ? Mystery. Then, suddenly, I thought of Rodney Clegg, and where there had been darkness I saw light.

The light, I must confess, was extremely disagreeable to me, at any rate in its first dawning. I experienced a much more violent return of that jealousy which had overtaken me when I heard Grace expressing her admiration of Rodney's character and talents. And with the jealousy a proportionately violent renewal of my desires. An object hitherto indifferent may suddenly be invested in our eyes with an inestimable value by the mere fact that it has passed irrevocably out of our power into the possession of some one else. The moment that I suspected Grace of having become Rodney's mistress I began to imagine myself passionately in love with her. I tortured myself with distressing thoughts of their felicity ; I cursed myself for having neglected opportunities that would never return. At one moment I even thought of rushing back to London, in the hope of snatching my now suddenly precious treasure out of Rodney's clutches. But the journey would have been expensive ; I was luckily short of money. In the end I decided to stay where I was. Time passed and my good sense returned. I realized that my passion was entirely imaginary, home-made, and self-suggested. I pictured to myself what would have happened if I had returned to London under its influence. Burning with artificial flames, I should have burst dramatically into Grace's presence, only to discover, when I was actually with her, that I was not in love with her at all. Imaginary love can only flourish at a distance from its object ; reality confines the fancy and puts it in its place. I had imagined myself unhappy because Grace had given herself to Rodney ; but the situation, I perceived, would have been infinitely more distressing if I had returned, had succeeded in capturing her for myself, and then discovered that, much as I liked and charming as I found her, I did not love her.

It was deplorable, no doubt, that she should have been taken in by a charlatan like Rodney ; it was a proof of bad taste on her part that she had not preferred to worship me, hopelessly, with an unrequited passion. Still, it was her business and in no way mine. If she felt that she could be happy with Rodney, well then, poor idiot ! let her be happy. And so on. It was with reflections such as these that I solaced myself back into the indifference of a mere spectator. When Herbert turned up a few days later at my hotel, I was able to ask him, quite without agitation, for news of Grace.

' Oh, she 's just the same as usual,' said Herbert.

Crass fool ! I pressed him. ' Doesn't she go out more than she used to ? ' I asked. ' To dances and that sort of thing ? I had heard rumours that she was becoming so social.'

' She may be,' said Herbert. ' I hadn't noticed anything in particular.'

It was hopeless. I saw that if I wanted to know anything, I should have to use my own eyes and my own judgment. Meanwhile, I wrote to tell her how glad I was to know that she was happy and amusing herself. She replied with a long and very affected essay about ' pleasures.' After that, the correspondence flagged.

A few months later—I had just returned to London—there was a party at Rodney's studio, at which I was present. Rodney's latest masterpiece looked down from an easel set up at the end of the long room. It was an amusingly indecent pastiche of the Douanier Rousseau. 'Wedding,' the composition was called ; and it represented a nuptial party, the bride and bridegroom at the centre, the relatives standing or sitting round them, grouped as though before the camera of a provincial photographer. In the background a draped column, palpably cardboard ; a rustic bridge ; fir-trees with snow and, in the sky, a large pink dirigible. The only eccentric feature of the picture was that, while the bridegroom and the other gentlemen of the party were duly clothed in black Sunday best, the ladies, except for boots and hats, were naked. The best critics were of opinion that 'Wedding' represented the highest flight, up to date, of Rodney's genius. He was asking four hundred and fifty pounds for it ; a few days later, I was told, he actually got them.

Under the stonily fixed regard of the nuptial group Rodney's guests were diverting themselves. The usual people sat, or stood, or sprawled about, drinking white wine or whisky. Two of the young ladies had come dressed identically in the shirts and black velvet trousers of Gavarni's *débardeurs*. Another was smoking a small briar pipe. As I came into the room I heard a young man saying in a loud, truculent voice : 'We're absolutely modern, we are. Anybody can have my wife, so far as I'm concerned. I

don't care. She's free. And I'm free.
That's what I call modern.'

I could not help wondering why he should
call it modern. To me it rather seemed
primeval—almost pre-human. Love, after all,
is the new invention ; promiscuous lust geologically old-fashioned. The really modern
people, I reflected, are the Brownings.

I shook hands with Rodney.

' Don't be too contemptuous of our simple
London pleasures,' he said.

I smiled ; it amused me to hear on his lips
the word with which Grace's letters had made
me so familiar.

' As good as the pleasures of Paris, any day,'
I answered, looking round the room. Through
the crowd, I caught sight of Grace.

With an air of being spiritually and physically at home, she was moving from group to
group. In Rodney's rooms, I could see, she
was regarded as the hostess. The mistress of
the house, in the left-handed sense of the word.
(A pity, I reflected, that I could not share that
little joke with Rodney ; he would have enjoyed it so much, about any one else.) In the
intervals of conversation I curiously observed
her ; I compared the Grace before my eyes
with the remembered image of Grace as I first
knew her. That trick of swaying as she
walked—rather as a serpent sways to the piping
of the charmer—that was new. So, too, was

the carriage of the hands—the left on the hip, the right held breast-high, palm upwards, with a cigarette between the fingers. And when she put the cigarette to her lips, she had a novel way of turning up her face and blowing the smoke almost perpendicularly into the air, which was indescribably dashing and Bohemian. Haughty milady had vanished to be replaced by a new kind of aristocrat—the gay, terrible, beyond-good-and-evil variety.

From time to time snatches of her talk came to my ears. Gossip, invariably scandalous ; criticisms of the latest exhibitions of pictures ; recollections or anticipations of ' perfect parties '—these seemed to be the principal topics, all of them, in Grace's mouth, quite unfamiliar to me. But the face, the vague-featured face of the nice but ugly little girl, the bewildered eyes, the occasional smile, so full of sweetness and a dim benevolence—these were still the same. And when I overheard her airily saying to one of her new friends of I know not what common acquaintance, ' She 's almost too hospitable—positively keeps open bed, you know,' I could have burst out laughing, so absurdly incongruous with the face, the eyes, the smile, so palpably borrowed and not her own did the smart words seem.

Meanwhile, at the table, Rodney was doing one of his famous ' non-stop ' drawings—a figure, a whole scene rendered in a single line, without lifting the pencil from the paper. He was the centre of an admiring group.

' Isn't it too enchanting ? '

' Exquisite ! '

' Ravishing ! '

The words exploded laughingly all around him.

' There,' said Rodney, straightening himself up.

The paper was handed round for general inspection. Incredibly ingenious it was, that drawing, in a single sinuous line, of a fight between a bull and three naked female toreros. Every one applauded, called for more.

' What shall I do next ? ' asked Rodney.

' Trick cyclists,' somebody suggested.

' Stale, stale,' he objected.

' Self portrait.'

Rodney shook his head. ' Too vain.'

' Adam and Eve.'

' Or why not Salmon and Gluckstein ? ' suggested some one else.

' Or the twelve Apostles.'

' I have it,' shouted Rodney, waving his pencil. ' King George and Queen Mary.'

He bent over his scribbling block, and in a couple of minutes had produced a one-line portrait of the Britannic Majesties. There was a roar of laughter.

It was Grace who brought me the paper.

82

'Isn't he wonderful?' she said, looking at me with a kind of eager anxiety, as though she were anxious to have my commendation of her choice, my sacerdotal benediction.

I had only seen her once, for a brief un-intimate moment, since my return. We had not mentioned Rodney's name. But this evening, I saw, she was taking me into her confidence ; she was begging me, without words, but none the less eloquently, to tell her that she had done well. I don't exactly know why she should have desired my blessing. She seemed to regard me as a sort of old, grey-haired, avuncular Polonius. (Not a very flattering opinion, considering that I was several years younger than Rodney himself.) To her, my approval was the approval of embodied wisdom.

'Isn't he wonderful?' she repeated. 'Do you know of any other man now living, except perhaps Picasso, who could improvise a thing like that? For fun—as a game.'

I handed the paper back to her. The day before, as it happened, finding myself in the neighbourhood, I had dropped in on Rodney at his studio. He was drawing when I entered, but, seeing me, had closed his book and come to meet me. While we were talking, the plumber called and Rodney had left the studio to give some instructions on the spot, in the bathroom. I got up and strolled about

the room, looking at the latest canvases.
Perhaps too inquisitively, I opened the note-
book in which he had been drawing when I
entered. The book was blank but for the
first three or four pages. These were covered
with ' non-stop ' drawings. I counted seven
distinct versions of the bull with the female
toreros, and five, a little corrected and im-
proved each time, of King George and Queen
Mary. I wondered at the time why he should
be practising this peculiar kind of art ; but
feeling no urgent curiosity about the subject,
I forgot, when he came back, to ask him.
Now I understood.

' Extraordinary,' I said to Grace, as I returned her the paper. ' Really extraordinary ! '

Her smile of gratitude and pleasure was so
beautiful that I felt quite ashamed of myself
for knowing Rodney's little secret.

Grace and I both lived in Kensington ; it was
I who drove her home when the party was over.

' Well, that was great fun,' I said, as we
settled into the taxi.

We had driven past a dozen lamp-posts
before she spoke.

' You know, Dick,' she said, ' I 'm so happy.'

She laid her hand on my knee ; and for lack
of any possible verbal comment, I gently
patted it. There was another long silence.

' But why do you despise us all ? ' she asked,
turning on me suddenly.

'But when did I ever say I despised you?'
I protested.

'Oh, one needn't say such things. They proclaim themselves.'

I laughed, but more out of embarrassment than because I was amused. 'A woman's intuition, what?' I said facetiously. 'But you've really got too much of it, my dear Grace. You intuit things that aren't there at all.'

'But you despise us all the same.'

'I don't. Why should I?'

'Exactly. Why should you?'

'Why?' I repeated.

'For the sake of what?' she went on quickly. 'And in comparison with what do you find our ways so despicable? I'll tell you. For the sake of something impossible and inhuman. And in comparison with something that doesn't exist. It's stupid, when there's real life with all its pleasures.' That word again—Rodney's word! It seemed to me that she had a special, almost unctuous tone when she pronounced it. 'So delightful. So rich and varied. But you turn up your nose and find it all vapid and empty. Isn't it true?' she insisted.

'No,' I answered. I could have told her that life doesn't necessarily mean parties with white wine and whisky, social stunts, fornication and chatter. I might have told her;

but however studiously I might have generalized, it was obvious that my remarks would be
interpreted (quite correctly, indeed) as a set
of disparaging personalities. And I didn't
want to quarrel with Grace or offend her. And
besides, when all was said, I did go to Rodney's
parties. I was an accomplice. The knock-
about amused me ; I found it hard to deny
myself the entertainment. My objection was
only theoretical ; I did what I denounced.
I had no right to strike pontifical attitudes and
condemn. ' No, of course it isn't true,' I
repeated.

Grace sighed. ' Of course, I can't really
expect you to admit it,' she said. ' But bless
you,' she added with a forced and unnatural
gaiety, ' I don't mind being despised. When
one is rich, one can afford the luxury of being
disapproved of. And I am rich, you know.
Happiness, pleasures—I 've got everything.
And after all,' she went on, with a certain
argumentative truculence in her voice, ' I 'm
a woman. What do I care for your ridiculous
masculine standards. I do what I like, what
amuses me.' The quotation from Rodney
rang a little false, I thought. There was a
silence.

I wondered what John Peddley thought
about it all, or whether any suspicion of what
was happening had yet penetrated the horny
carapace of his insensitiveness.

And as though she were answering my un-spoken question, Grace began again with a new seriousness. 'And there's my other life, parallel. It doesn't make any difference to that, you know. Doesn't touch it. I like John just as much as I did. And the children, of course.'

There was another long silence. All at once, I hardly know why, I felt profoundly sad. Listening to this young woman talking about her lover, I wished that I too were in love. Even the 'pleasures' glittered before my fancy with a new and tempting brilliance. My life seemed empty. I found myself thinking of the melody of the Countess's song in *Figaro : Dove sono i bei momenti di dolcezza e di piacer ?*

That Grace's adventure made little or no difference to her other life, I had an oppor-tunity of judging for myself in the course of a subsequent week-end with the Peddleys in Kent. John was there—'in great form,' as he put it himself ; and Grace, and the children, and Grace's father and mother. Nothing could have been more domestic and less like Rodney's party, less 'modern.' Indeed, I should be justified in writing that last word without its inverted commas. For there was something extraordinarily remote and uncon-temporary about the whole household. The children were geologically remote in their

childishness—only a little beyond the pithe-
canthropus stage. And Peddley was like a
star, separated from the world by the un-
bridgeable gulfs of his egoism and unawareness. The subjects of his discourse might be
contemporary ; but spiritually, none the less,
he was timeless, an inhabitant of blank and
distant space. As for Grace's parents, they
were only a generation away ; but, goodness
knows, that was far enough. They had
opinions about socialism and sexual morality,
and gentlemen, and what ought or ought not
to be done by the best people—fixed, un-
alterable, habit-ingrained and by now almost
instinctive opinions that made it impossible
for them to understand or forgive the contemporary world.

This was especially true of Grace's mother.
She was a big, handsome woman of about
fifty-five, with the clear ringing voice of one
who has been accustomed all her life to give
orders. She busied herself in doing good
works and generally keeping the poor in their
places. Unlike her husband, who had a
touch of Peddley's star-like remoteness, she
was very conscious of contemporaneity and,
consequently, very loud and frequent in her
denunciations of it.

Grace's father, who had inherited money,
filled his leisure by farming a small estate un-
profitably, sitting on committees, and reading

Persian, an acquirement of which, in his quiet way, he was very proud. It was a strangely disinterested hobby. He had never been to Persia and had not the slightest intention of ever going. He was quite uninterested in Persian literature or history, and was just as happy reading a Persian cookery book as the works of Hafiz or Rumi. What he liked was the language itself. He enjoyed the process of reading the unfamiliar letters, of looking up the words in the dictionary. For him, Persian was a kind of endlessly complicated jigsaw puzzle. He studied it solely for the sake of killing time and in order not to think. A dim, hopeless sort of man was Mr. Comfrey. And he had an irritating way of looking at you over the top of his spectacles with a puzzled expression, as though he had not understood what you meant ; which, indeed, was generally the case. For Mr. Comfrey was very slow of mind and made up for his knowledge of Persian by the most extraordinary ignorance of almost all other subjects under the sun.

' Say that again,' he would say, when his incomprehension was too complete.

How strange, how utterly fantastic it seemed, that week-end. I felt as though I had been suddenly lifted out of the contemporary world and plunged into a kind of limbo.

John Peddley's latest subject was the Einstein theory.

'It's so simple,' he assured us the first evening, between the soup and the fish. 'I don't pretend to be a mathematician or anything like one ; but I understand it perfectly. All that it needs is a little common sense.' And for the next half-hour the common sense came braying out, as though from the mouth of a trombone.

Grace's father looked at him dubiously over the top of his spectacles.

'Say that again, will you ? ' he said, after every second sentence.

And John Peddley was only too delighted to oblige.

At the other end of the table, Grace and her mother were discussing the children, their clothes, characters, education, diseases. I longed to join in their conversation. But the simple domesticities were not for me. I was a man ; John Peddley and the intellect were my portion. Reluctantly, I turned back towards my host.

'What I'd like you to explain,' Grace's father was saying, 'is just exactly how time can be at right angles to length, breadth, and thickness. Where precisely does it come in ? ' With two forks and a knife he indicated the three spatial dimensions. 'Where do you find room for another right angle ? '

And John Peddley set himself to explain. It was terrible.

Meanwhile, at my other ear, Grace's mother had begun to talk about the undesirable neighbours who had taken the house next to theirs on Campden Hill. A man and a woman, living together, unmarried. And the garden behind the houses was the common property of all the householders. What a situation ! Leaving Peddley and the old gentleman to find room for the fourth right angle, I turned definitively to the ladies. For my benefit, Grace's mother began the horrid story again from the beginning. I was duly sympathetic.

Once, for a moment, I caught Grace's eye. She smiled at me, she almost imperceptibly raised her eyebrows. That little grimace was deeply significant. In the first months of our friendship, I had often seen her in the company of her father and mother, and her bearing, on these occasions, had always impressed me. I had never met a young woman of the generation which had come to maturity during the war who was so perfectly at ease with her elders, so unconstrainedly at home in their moral and mental atmosphere as was Grace. She had taken her father and mother entirely for granted, had regarded their views of life as the obvious, natural views of every sane human being. That embarrassment which —in these days, more perhaps than at any other period—afflicts young people when in the presence of their elders had never, so far as I had observed, touched Grace. This smile of apologetic and slightly contemptuous indulgence, this raising of the eyebrows, were symptomatic of a change. Grace had become contemporary, even (in inverted commas) ' modern.'

Outwardly, however, there was no change. The two worlds were parallel ; they did not meet. They did not meet, even when Rodney came to dine *en famille*, even when John accompanied his wife to one of Rodney's less aggressively ' artistic ' (which in inverted commas means very much the same as ' modern ') evening parties. Or perhaps it would be truer to say that Rodney's world met John's, but John's did not meet Rodney's. Only if Rodney had been a Zulu and his friends Chinese would John have noticed that they were at all different from the people he was used to meeting. The merely spiritual differences which distinguished them were too small for his notice. He moved through life surrounded by his own atmosphere ; only the most glaring lights could penetrate that half opaque and intensely refractive medium. For John, Rodney and his friends were just people, like everybody else ; people who could be button-holed and talked to about the Swiss banking system and Einstein's theory, and the rationing of sugar. Sometimes, it was true,

they seemed to him rather frivolous ; their
manners, sometimes, struck him as rather
unduly brusque ; and John had even remarked
that they were sometimes rather coarse-spoken
in the presence of ladies—or, if they happened
to be ladies themselves, in the presence of
gentlemen.

' Curious, these young people,' he said to
me, after an evening at Rodney's studio.
' Curious.' He shook his head. ' I don't
know that I quite understand them.'

Through a rift in his atmosphere he had
caught a glimpse of the alien world beyond ;
he had seen something, not refracted, but as
it really was. But John was quite incurious ;
careless of its significance, he shut out the unfamiliar vision.

' I don't know what your opinion about
modern art may be,' he went on, disappointing
me of his comments on modern people. ' But
what I always say is this.'

And he said it, copiously.

Modern art became another gramophone
record added to his repertory. That was the
net result of his meeting with Rodney and
Rodney's friends.

For the next few months I saw very little
either of Grace or of Rodney. I had met
Catherine, and was too busy falling in love to
do or think of anything else. We were
married towards the close of 1921, and

life became for me, gradually, once more normal.

From the first Catherine and Grace were friends. Grace admired Catherine for her coolness, her quiet efficiency, her reliableness ; admired and liked her. Catherine's affection for Grace was protective and elder-sisterly ; and at the same time, she found Grace slightly comic. Affections are not impaired by being tempered with a touch of benevolent laughter. Indeed, I would almost be prepared to risk a generalization and say that all true affections are tempered with laughter. For affection implies intimacy ; and one cannot be intimate with another human being without discovering something to laugh at in his or her character. Almost all the truly virtuous characters in fiction are also slightly ridiculous ; perhaps that is because their creators were so fond of them. Catherine saw the joke—the rather pathetic joke—of Grace. But she liked her none the less ; perhaps, even, the more. For the joke was appealing ; it was a certain childishness that raised the laugh.

At the time of my marriage, Grace was acting the eternally feminine part more fervently than ever. She had begun to dress very smartly and rather eccentrically, and was generally unpunctual ; not very unpunctual (she was by nature too courteous for that), but just enough to be able to say that she was horribly late, but that she couldn't help it ; it was in her nature—her woman's nature. She blamed Catherine for dressing too sensibly.

' You must be gayer in your clothes,' she insisted, ' more fantastic and capricious. It 'll make you *feel* more fantastic. You think too masculinely.'

And to encourage her in thinking femininely, she gave her six pairs of white kid gloves, marvellously piped with coloured leather and with fringed and intricately scalloped gauntlets. But perhaps the most feminine and fantastic thing about them was the fact that they were several sizes too small for Catherine's hand.

Grace had become a good deal more loquacious of late and her style of conversation had changed. Like her clothes, it was more fantastic than in the past. The principle on which she made conversation was simple : she said whatever came into her head. And into that vague, irresponsible head of hers the oddest things would come. A phantasmagoria of images, changing with every fresh impression or as the words of her interlocutor called up new associations, was for ever dancing across her field of mental vision. She put into words whatever she happened to see at any given moment. For instance, I might mention the musician Palestrina.

' Yes, yes,' Grace would say, ' what a marvellous composer ! ' Then, reacting to the Italian reference, she would add in the same breath : ' And the way they positively *drink* the macaroni.  Like those labels that come out of the mouth of caricatures.  You know.'

Sometimes I did know.  I skipped over the enormous ellipses in this allusive thinking and caught the reference.  Sometimes, when the association of her ideas was too exclusively private, I was left uncomprehending.  The new technique was rather disconcerting, but it was always amusing, in a way.  The unexpectedness of her remarks, the very nonsensicality of them, surprised one into finding them witty.

As a child, Grace had been snubbed when she talked in this random, fantastic fashion. ' Talk sense,' her governesses had said severely, when she told them during the geography lesson that she didn't like South America because it looked like a boiled leg of mutton. ' Don't be silly.'  Grace was taught to be ashamed of her erratic fancy.  She tried to talk sense—sense as governesses understand it—found it very difficult, and relapsed into silence.  Peddley was even more sensible, in the same style, than the governesses themselves ; devastatingly sensible.  He was incapable of understanding fancy.  If Grace had ever told Peddley why she didn't like South America, he would have been puzzled, he would have asked her to explain herself.  And

learning that it was the mutton-like shape of
the continent on the map that prejudiced
Grace against it, he would have given her
statistics of South America's real dimensions,
would have pointed out that it extended from
the tropics almost into the antarctic circle, that
it contained the largest river and some of the
highest mountains in the world, that Brazil
produced coffee and the Argentine beef, and
that consequently, in actual fact, it was not in
the very least like a boiled leg of mutton.
With Peddley, Grace's only resources were
laboriously talked sense or complete silence.

In Rodney's circle, however, she found that
her gift of nonsense was appreciated and
applauded. An enthusiast for the ' fantastic '
and the ' feminine,' Rodney encouraged her
to talk at random, as the spirit of associative
fancy might move her. Diffidently at first,
Grace let herself go ; her conversation
achieved an immediate success. Her un-
stitched, fragmentary utterances were regarded
as the last word in modern wit. People repeated her *bons mots*. A little bewildered by
what had happened, Grace suddenly found
herself in the movement, marching at the very
head of the forces of contemporaneity. In
the eighteenth century, when logic and science
were the fashion, women tried to talk like
the men. The twentieth century has reversed
the process. Rodney did Grace the honour

of appropriating to himself the happiest of her extravagances.

Success made Grace self-confident ; and confident, she went forward triumphantly to further successes. It was a new and intoxicating experience for her. She lived in a state of chronic spiritual tipsiness.

'How stupid people are not to be happy !' she would say, whenever we discussed these eternal themes.

To Catherine, who had taken my place as a confidant—my place and a much more intimate, more confidential place as well—she talked about love and Rodney.

'I can't think why people manage to make themselves unhappy about love,' she said. 'Why can't everybody love gaily and freely, like us ? Other people's love seems to be all black and clotted, like Devonshire cream made of ink. Ours is like champagne. That's what love ought to be like : champagne. Don't you think so ?'

'I think I should prefer it to be like clear water,' said Catherine. To me, later on, she expressed her doubts. 'All this champagne and gaiety,' she said ; 'one can see that Rodney is a young man with a most wholesome fear of emotional entanglements.'

'We all knew that,' I said. 'You didn't imagine, I suppose, that he was in love with her?'

'I hoped,' said Catherine.

'Because you didn't know Rodney. Now you do. Champagne—you have the formula. The problem is Grace.'

Was she really in love with him ? Catherine and I discussed the question. I was of opinion that she was.

'When Rodney flutters off,' I said, ' she 'll be left there, broken.'

Catherine shook her head. 'She only imagines she 's in love,' she insisted. ' It 's the huge excitement of it all that makes her happy ; that, and the novelty of it, and her sense of importance, and her success. Not any deep passion for Rodney. She may think it 's a passion—a champagnish passion, if you like. But it isn't really. There 's no passion ; only champagne. It was his prestige and her boredom that made her fall to him originally. And now it 's her success and the fun of it that make her stick to him.'

Events were to show that Catherine was right, or at least more nearly right than I. But before I describe these events, I must tell how it was that Kingham re-entered my world.

It was I who took the first step to end our ridiculous quarrel. I should have made the attempt earlier, if it had not been for Kingham's absence from Europe. A little while after our squabble he left, with a commission to write articles as he went, first for North Africa and thence for the further East. I heard of him once or twice from people who had seen him at Tunis, at Colombo, at Canton. And I read the articles, the admirably original articles, as they appeared at intervals in the paper which had commissioned them. But direct communication with him I had none. I did not write ; for I was uncertain, to begin with, if my letter would ever reach him. And in any case, even if we had made up our quarrel by letter, what good would that have been ? Reconciliations across eight thousand miles of space are never very satisfactory. I waited till I heard of his return and then wrote him a long letter. Three days later he was sitting at our dinner-table.

' This is good,' he said, ' this is very good.' He looked this way and that, quickly, taking in everything—the furniture, the books, Catherine, me—with his bright, quick eyes. ' Definitely settled.'

' Oh, not so definitely as all that, let us hope.' I laughed in Catherine's direction.

' I envy you,' he went on. ' To have got hold of something fixed, something solid and absolute—that 's wonderful. Domestic love, marriage—after all, it 's the nearest thing to an absolute that we can achieve, practically. And it takes on more value, when you 've been rambling round the world for a bit, as I have. The world proves to you that nothing has any meaning except in relation to something else.

Good, evil, justice, civilization, cruelty, beauty.
You think you know what these words mean.
And perhaps you do know, in Kensington.
But go to India or China. You don't know
anything there. It 's uncomfortable at first ;
but then, how exciting ! And how much
more copiously and multifariously you begin
to live ! But precisely for that reason you feel
the need for some sort of fixity and definition,
some kind of absolute, not merely of the
imagination, but in actual life. That 's where
love comes in, and domesticity. Not to
mention God and Death and the Immortality
of the Soul and all the rest. When you live
narrowly and snugly, those things seem absurd
and superfluous. You don't even appreciate
your snugness. But multiply yourself with
travelling, knock the bottom out of all your
old certainties and prejudices and habits of
thought ; then you begin to see the real significance of domestic snugness, you appreciate
the reality and importance of the other fixities.'

He spoke with all his old passionate eager-
ness. His eyes had the same feverish, almost
unearthly brightness. His face, which had
been smooth and pale when I saw it last, was
burnt by the sun and lined. He looked more
mature, tougher and stronger than in the past.

' Yes, I envy you,' he repeated.

' Then why don't you get married yourself ? '
asked Catherine.

Kingham laughed. 'Why not, indeed? You'd better ask Dick. He knows me well enough to answer, I should think.'

'No, tell us yourself,' I said.

Kingham shook his head. 'It would be a case of cruelty to animals,' he said enigmatically, and began to talk about something else.

'I envy you,' he said again, later that same evening, when Catherine had gone to bed and we were alone together. 'I envy you. But you don't deserve what you've got. You haven't earned your right to a fixed domestic absolute, as I have. I've realized, intimately and personally realized, the flux and the interdependence and the relativity of things ; consequently I know and appreciate the meaning and value of fixity. But you—you're domestic just as you're moral ; you're moral and domestic by nature, unconsciously, instinctively, without having known the opposites which give these attitudes their significance— like a worker bee, in fact ; like a damned cabbage that just grows because it can't help it.'

I laughed. 'I like the way you talk about flux and relativity,' I said, 'when you yourself are the fixed, unchanging antithesis of these things. The same old Kingham ! Why, you're a walking fixity ; you're the Absolute in flesh and blood. How well I know those dear old home truths, for example !'

'But that doesn't prevent their being true,'

he insisted, laughing, but at the same time rather annoyed by what I had said. 'And besides, I *have* changed. My views about everything are quite different. A sensitive man can't go round the world and come back with the same philosophy of life as the one he started with.'

'But he can come back with the same temperament, the same habits of feeling, the same instinctive reactions.'

Kingham ran his fingers through his hair and repeated his petulant laughter. 'Well, I suppose he can,' he admitted reluctantly.

I was only too well justified in what I had said. A few days of renewed intimacy were enough to convince me that Kingham preserved all his old love of a scene, that he enjoyed as much as ever the luxury of a hot emotional bath. He burst in on me one morning, distracted with fury, to tell me about a violent quarrel he had had the previous evening with some insignificant young undergraduate—rather tipsy at that—who had told him (with considerable insight, I must admit, in spite of his tipsiness) that he, Kingham, was either insincere or hysterical.

'And the awful thing is that he may be right,' he added, when he had finished his story. 'Perhaps I *am* insincere.' Restlessly, he walked about the room. From time to time he withdrew a hand from the pocket into

which it was deeply plunged and made a
gesture, or ran the fingers through his hair.
'Perhaps I 'm just a little comedian,' he went
on, 'just a mouther of words, a ranter.' The
self-laceration hurt him, but he enjoyed the
pain. 'Do I really feel things deeply ?' he
went on speculating. 'Or do I just deceive
myself into believing that I care ? Is it all
a mere lie ?' The operation continued in-
terminably.

The tipsy undergraduate had diagnosed
insincerity or hysteria. It was in my power
to relieve Kingham of his haunting fear of
insincerity by assuring him that the second of
these alternatives was the more correct. But
I doubted the efficacy of the consolation ; and
besides I had no desire for a quarrel. I held
my tongue.

I did not make Kingham known to Grace ;
for knowing that he had a passionate and rooted
dislike of Rodney, I was afraid that, in spite of
my preliminary warnings (or even precisely
because of them, for the sake of creating an
intolerably unpleasant situation) he might
burst out, in Grace's presence, into some
violent denunciation of her lover. It was a
risk that was not worth running. And besides, I did not imagine that they would get on
well together. We were intimate with both ;
but we kept them, so to speak, in separate
water-tight compartments of our intimacy.

One day, when I came home to dinner, I was greeted by Catherine with a piece of news.

'Rodney's being unfaithful,' she said. 'Poor little Grace was here for tea to-day. She pretends not to mind—to be very modern and hard and gay about it. But I could see that she was dreadfully upset.'

'And who's the lucky lady?' I asked.

'Mrs. Melilla.'

'A step up in the world.' I thought of the emeralds and the enormous pearls, which added lustre to the already dazzling Jewish beauty of Mrs. Melilla. 'He'll be in the baronetcy and peerage soon.'

'What a pig!' said Catherine indignantly. 'I'm so dreadfully sorry for poor Grace.'

'But according to your theory, she isn't really in love with him.'

'No, she isn't,' said Catherine. 'Not *really*. But she thinks she is. And she'll think so much more, of course, now that he's leaving her. And besides, she has put so many of her eggs into his basket ; this smashes them all. She'd committed herself body and soul to Rodney and Rodneyism. This affair with Rodney gave sense to her whole existence. Can't you see that?'

'Perfectly.' I remembered the days when Grace had seen herself as a musical critic and how cruelly I had murdered this comforting vision of herself by my little practical joke about the player of Rachmaninoff. A much more significant, much more intimately cherished dream was being murdered now.

She did her best, as Catherine had said, to be very ' modern ' about it. I saw her a few days later at one of Rodney's parties ; she was smoking a great many cigarettes, drinking glass after glass of white wine and talking more wildly than ever. Her dress was a close-fitting sheath of silver tissue, designed so as to make the wearer look almost naked. Fatigued with sleeplessness, her eyes were circled with dark, bruise-coloured rings ; seen in conjunction with the bright, unnatural red of her rouged cheeks and lips, these dark circles looked as though they had been painted on with a fard, to heighten the brilliance of the eyes, to hint provocatively at voluptuous fatigues and amorous vigils. She was having a great success and her admirers had never been more numerous. She flirted outrageously with all of them. Even when she was talking with me, she seemed to find it necessary to shoot languorous sidelong glances ; to lean towards me, as though offering her whole person to my desires. But looking at her, I could see, under the fard, only the face of the nice but rather ugly little girl ; it seemed, I thought, more than usually pathetic.

Rodney sat down at the table to do his usual non-stop drawing.

' What shall it be ? ' he asked.

' Draw Jupiter and *all* his mistresses,' cried Grace, who was beginning to be rather tipsy. ' Europa and Leda and Semele and Danae,' she clapped her hands at each name, ' and Io and . . . and Clio and Dio and Scio and Fi-fio and O-my-Eyeo. . . .'

The jest was not a very good one. But as most of Rodney's guests had drunk a good deal of wine and all were more or less intoxicated by the convivial atmosphere of a successful party, there was a general laugh. Grace began to laugh too, almost hysterically. It was a long time before she could control herself.

Rodney, who had made no preparations for improvising a picture of Jove's mistresses, found an excuse for rejecting the suggestion. He ended by drawing Mrs. Eddy pursued by a satyr.

Deserted by Rodney, Grace tried to pretend that it was she who was the deserter. The rôle of the capricious wanton seemed to her more in harmony with the Rodneyan conception of the eternal feminine as well as less humiliating than that of the victim. Provocatively, promiscuously, she flirted. In those first days of her despair she would, I believe, have accepted the advances of almost any tolerably presentable man. Masterman, for example, or Gane the journalist, or Levitski—it was

one of those three, I surmised, judging by
what I saw at the party, who would succeed
to Rodney's felicity, and that very soon.

The day after the party, Grace paid another
visit to Catherine. She brought a small
powder-puff as a present. In return, she
asked, though not in so many words, for comfort, advice, and above all for approval. In
a crisis, on the spur of the moment, Grace
could be rashly and unreflectingly impulsive ;
but when there was time to think, when it was
a question of deliberately planning she was
timorous, she hated to stand alone and take
responsibilities. She liked to know that the
part in which she saw herself was approved
of by some trustworthy judge. The powder-
puff was a bribe and an argument ; an argument in favour of the eternal feminine, with
all that that connoted, a bribe for the judge,
an appeal to her affection, that she might
approve of Grace's sentiments and conduct.

Grace put her case. ' The mistake people
make,' she said, ' is getting involved, like the
man on the music-halls who does that turn
with the fly-paper. I refuse to be involved ;
that 's my principle. I think one ought to
be heartless and just amuse oneself, that 's all.
Not worry about anything else.'

' But do you think one can really be amused
if one doesn't worry and takes things heart-
lessly ? ' asked Catherine. ' *Really* amused,

I mean. Happy, if you 'll permit me to use an old-fashioned word. Can one be happy ? ' She thought of Levitski, of Gane and Masterman.

Grace was silent ; perhaps she too was thinking of them. Then, making an effort, ' Yes, yes,' she said with a kind of obstinate, determined gaiety, ' one can ; of course one can.'

I was at the Queen's Hall that afternoon. Coming out, when the concert was over, I caught sight of Kingham in the issuing crowd.

' Come home for a late cup of tea and stay to dinner.'

' All right,' he said.

We climbed on to a bus and rode westward. The sun had just set. Low down in the sky in front of us there were streaks of black and orange cloud, and above them a pale, watery-green expanse, limpid and calm up to the zenith. We rode for some time in silence, watching the lovely death of yet another of our days.

' It 's all very well,' said Kingham at last, indicating these western serenities with a gesture of his fine, expressive hand, ' it 's all very well, no doubt, for tired business men. Gives them comfort, I dare say ; makes them feel agreeably repentant for the swindles they 've committed during the day, and all that. Oh, it 's full of uplift, I 've no doubt.

But I don't happen to be a tired business man. It just makes me sick.'

' Come, come,' I protested.

He wouldn't listen to me. ' I won't have Gray's ' Elegy ' rammed down my throat,' he said. ' What I feel like is *The Marriage of Heaven and Hell*, or *Zarathustra*, or the *Chants de Maldoror*.'

' Well, all that I can suggest' (I suggested it mildly) ' is that you should travel inside the bus and not look at the sunset.'

' Ass ! ' he said contemptuously.

We came in, to find Grace still sitting there, over the tea-cups, with Catherine. I was annoyed ; still, there was nothing to be done about it. I introduced Kingham. All unconsciously, I was playing Pandarus for the second time.

My sources for the history of Grace's second love affair are tolerably copious. To begin with, I had opportunities of personally observing it, during a considerable part of its duration. I heard much, too, from Kingham himself. For Kingham was not at all a discreet lover. He was as little capable of being secretive about this class of experiences as about any other. He simply had to talk. Talking renewed and multiplied the emotions which he described. Talk even created new emotions—emotions which he had not felt at the time but which it occurred to him, when he was describing the scene, to think that he ought to have felt.   He had no scruples about projecting these *sentiments d'escalier* backwards, anachronistically, into his past experience, falsifying history for the sake of future drama. To his memories of a scene with Grace he would add emotional complications, so that the next scene might be livelier.   It was in the heat of talk that his finest emendations of history occurred to him.   The genuine, or at any rate the on the whole more genuine, story came to me through Catherine from Grace. It was to Catherine that, in moments of crisis (and this particular love affair was almost uninterruptedly a crisis) Grace came for solace and counsel.

The affair began with a misunderstanding. No sooner had Kingham entered the room than Grace, who had been talking quite simply and naturally with Catherine, put on her brazen ' modern ' manner of the party and began with a kind of desperate recklessness to demand the attention and provoke the desires of the newcomer.   She knew Kingham's name, of course, and all about him.   In Rodney's circle it was admitted, albeit with some reluctance, that the man had talent ; but he was deplored as a barbarian.

' He 's one of those tiresome people,' I once heard Rodney complain, ' who will talk about their soul—and your soul, which is almost worse. Terribly Salvation Army. One wouldn't be surprised to see him on Sundays in Hyde Park telling people what they ought to do to be saved.'

At the sight of him, Grace had felt, no doubt, that it would be amusing to bring this curious wild animal to heel and make it do tricks. (It did not occur to her that it might be she who would be doing the tricks.) Kingham was a quarry worthy of any huntswoman. Still, I believe that she would have flirted as outrageously with almost any stranger. This provocative attitude of hers—an attitude which might be described as one of chronic and universal unfaithfulness—was her retort to unkind fate and unfaithful Rodney. She wanted to capture a new lover—several lovers, even—in order to prove to Rodney, to the world at large and above all, surely, to herself, that she was modern, knew how to take love lightly and gaily, as the most exquisite of entertainments, and that, in a word, she didn't care a pin. In another woman, this promiscuous flirtatiousness might have been distasteful, detestable even. But there was, in Grace, a certain fundamental innocence that rendered what ought, by all the rules, to have been the most reprehensible of actions entirely harmless. Text-book moralists would have called her bad, when in fact she was merely pathetic and a trifle comic. The text-books assign to every

action its place in the moral hierarchy ; the
text-book moralists judge men exclusively by
their actions. The method is crude and un-
scientific. For in reality certain characters have
power to sterilize a dirty action ; certain others
infect and gangrene actions which, according
to the book, should be regarded as clean. The
harshest judges are those who have been so
deeply hypnotized by the spell of the text-book
words, that they have become quite insensitive
to reality. They can think only of words—
' purity,' ' vice,' ' depravity,' ' duty ' ; the
existence of men and women escapes their
notice.

Grace, as I have said, possessed an innocence
which made nonsense of all the words which
might have been used to describe her actions.
To any one but a text-book theorist it was
obvious that the actions hardly mattered ; her
innocence remained intact. It was this same
innocence which enabled her to give utterance
—with perfect unconcern and a complete
absence of daring affectation — to those
scabrous sentiments, those more than scientific
expressions which were almost *de rigueur* in
the conversation of Rodney's circle. In a
foreign language one can talk of subjects, one
can unconcernedly use words, the uttering,
the mention of which in one's native idiom
would horribly embarrass. For Grace, all
these words, the most genuinely Old English,

all these themes, however intimately connected
by gossip with the names of known men and
women, were foreign and remote. Even the
universal language of coquettish gestures was
foreign to her ; she acted its provocations and
innuendoes with a frankness which would have
been shameless, if she had really known what
they meant. Kingham entered the room ;
she turned on him at once all her batteries of
looks and smiles—a bombardment of provocations. I knew Grace so well that, in my eyes,
the performance seemed merely absurd.
These smiles, these sidelong glances and
flutteringly dropped eyelids, this teasing
mockery by which she irritated Kingham into
paying attention to her, struck me as wholly
uncharacteristic of Grace and therefore ridiculous—above all, unconvincing. Yes, unconvincing. I could not believe that any one
could fail to see what Grace was really like.
Was it possible that Kingham didn't realize
just as well as I did that she was, in spirit, as in
features, just a nice little girl, pretending
without much success—particularly in this
rôle—to be grown up ?

It seemed to me incredible. But Kingham
was certainly taken in. He accepted her at
her face value of this particular moment—as an
aristocratically reckless hedonist in wanton
search of amusement, pleasure, excitement, and
power. To the dangerous siren he took her

to be, Kingham reacted with a mixed emotion that was half angry contempt, half amorous curiosity. On principle, Kingham violently disapproved of professional *femmes fatales*, sirens, vampires—all women, in fact, who make love and the subjugation of lovers the principal occupation of their lives. He thought it outrageous that self-respecting and useful men should suddenly find themselves at the mercy of these dangerous and irresponsible beings. What perhaps increased his moral indignation was the fact that he himself was constantly falling a victim to them. Youth, vitality, strong personality, frank and unbridled vice had irresistible attractions for him. He was drawn sometimes to the vulgarest possessors of these characteristics. He felt it an indignity, a humiliation (and yet, who knows ? perhaps with Kingham this sense of humiliation was only another attraction) ; but he was none the less unfailingly drawn. He resisted, but never quite firmly enough (that, after all, would have spoiled all the fun). He resisted, succumbed and was subjected. But it must be admitted that his love, however abject it might be in the first moment of his surrender, was generally a vengeance in itself. Kingham might suffer ; but he contrived in most cases to inflict as much suffering as he received. And while he, with a part of his spirit at any

rate, actually enjoyed pain, however acutely
and genuinely felt, the tormentors whom he in
his turn tormented were mostly quite normal
young women with no taste for the pleasures
of suffering. He got the best of it ; but he
regarded himself, none the less, as the victim,
and was consequently in a chronic state of
moral indignation.

This first meeting convinced Kingham that
Grace was the sort of woman she wanted to
persuade him (not to mention herself) that she
was—a vampire. Like many persons of weak
character and lacking in self-reliance, Grace
was often extraordinarily reckless. Passive
generally and acquiescent, she sometimes
committed herself wildly to the most extravagant courses of action—not from any
principle of decision, but because, precisely,
she did not know what decision was, because
she lacked the sense of responsibility, and was
incapable of realizing the irrevocable nature
of an act. She imagined that she could do
things irresponsibly and without committing
herself ; and feeling no inward sense of com-
mitment, she would embark on courses of
action which—externalized and become a part
of the great machine of the world—dragged
her, sometimes reluctant, sometimes willing,
but always ingenuously surprised, into situations the most bewilderingly unexpected. It
was this irresponsible impulsiveness of a

character lacking the power of making deliberate decisions (this coupled with her fatal capacity for seeing herself in any rôle that seemed, at the moment, attractive) that had made her at one moment a socialist canvasser at the municipal elections ; at another, an occasional opium smoker in that sordid and dangerous den near the Commercial Docks which Tim Masterman used to frequent; at another, though she was terrified of horses, a rider to hounds ; and at yet another—to her infinite distress ; but having light-heartedly insisted that she didn't know what modesty was, she couldn't draw back—the model for one of Levitski's nudes. And if she now threw herself at Kingham's head (just as, a few nights before, she had thrown herself at Masterman's, at Gane's, at Levitski's), it was irresponsibly, without considering what might be the results of her action, without even fully realizing that there would be any results at all. True, she saw herself as a ' modern ' young woman ; and her abandonment by Rodney had made her anxious, for the mere saving of her face, to capture a new lover, quickly. And yet it would be wrong to say that she had decided to employ coquettish provocations in order to get what she wanted. She had not decided anything ; for decision is deliberate and the fruit of calculation. She was just wildly indulging in action, in precisely the same way as she indulged in random speech, without thinking of what the deeds or the words committed her to. But whereas logical inconsistencies matter extremely little and false intellectual positions can easily be abandoned, the effects of action or of words leading to action are not so negligible. For action commits what is much more important than the intellect—the body. To get the bodily self out of a false position is a difficult and often painful business. Grace, the indecisive, the all too easily and lightly moved to action, had often found it so to her cost. But that did not prevent her from repeating her mistake. Experience never does.

Kingham, as I have said, took her for what she irresponsibly wanted him to believe she was. He was duly provoked by what had been meant to be provocative. To this sort of amorous teasing he was extraordinarily susceptible. So much so, indeed, that his interest in Grace was no great tribute to her style. It was enough that a woman should exhibit a certain lively, vampirish interest in him ; Kingham was almost certain to succumb to the attack. I remember one occasion in Paris when he was positively swept off his feet by the shrill, metallic sallies of an American chorus-girl from the Folies Bergères.

This first impression of Grace—as a ' modern,' dangerously provocative, actively

wanton vampire—persisted in Kingham's mind
and no evidence to the contrary could obliterate
it.    In the course of their first meeting, he had
taken up his emotional attitude towards her ;
and the attitude once taken, he would not shift
his ground, however palpable the proofs that
he was wrong.    Whether he ceased to be able
to use his intelligence and became incapable
of recognizing the facts that would have upset
his prejudices, or whether he deliberately shut
his eyes to what he did not wish to see, I do
not exactly know.    A powerful emotion had
the double effect, I surmise, of rendering him
at one and the same time stupid and most
ingeniously perverse.

'I think there's something really devilish
about the women of this generation,' he said
to me, in his intense, emphatic way, some two
or three days later.   'Something devilish,' he
repeated, 'really devilish.'   It was a trick of
his, in writing as well as in speech, to get hold
of a word and, if he liked the sound of it, work
it to death.

I laughed.   'Oh, come,' I protested.   'Do
you find Catherine, for example, so specially
diabolic ? '

'She isn't of this generation,' Kingham
answered.   'Spiritually, she doesn't belong
to it.'

I laughed again ; it was always difficult
arguing with Kingham.   You might think

you had him cornered ; you raised your logical cudgel to smash him. But while you were bringing it down, he darted out from beneath the stroke through some little trap door of his own discovery, clean out of the argument. It was impossible to prove him in the wrong, for the simple reason that he never remained long enough in any one intellectual position to be proved anything.

'No, not Catherine,' he went on, after a little pause. ' I was thinking of that Peddley woman.'

' Grace ? ' I asked in some astonishment. ' Grace devilish ? '

He nodded. ' Devilish,' he repeated with conviction. The word, I could see, had acquired an enormous significance for him. It was the core round which, at the moment, all his thoughts and feelings were crystallizing. All his universe was arranging itself in patterns round the word ' devilish,' round the idea of devilishness in general, and Grace's devilishness in particular.

I protested. ' Of all the un-devilish people I 've ever known,' I said, ' Grace seems to me the most superlatively so.'

' You don't know her,' he retorted.

' But I 've known her for years.'

' Not really known,' insisted Kingham, diving through another of his little trap doors out of the argument. ' You 've never inspired

her with one of her devilish concupiscences.'
(I thought of Grace and could not help smiling ; the smile exasperated Kingham.) 'Grin
away,' he said. ' Imagine you 're omniscient,
if it gives you any pleasure. All I say is this:
she 's never tried to hunt you down.'

' I suppose you mean that she was rather
stupidly flirtatious the other evening,' I said.

Kingham nodded. ' It was devilish,' he
said softly, more for himself than for me.
' Devilish concupiscence.'

' But I assure you,' I went on, ' that business
the other night was all mere silliness. She 's
childish, not devilish. She still sees herself in
terms of Rodney Clegg, that 's all. And she
wants to pretend, now that he 's deserted her,
that she doesn't care. I 'm not sure, indeed,
that she doesn't want to make us believe that
it was she who deserted him. That 's why
she wants to get hold of another lover quickly
—for the sake of her prestige. But as for
devilishness—why, the idea 's simply absurd.
She isn't definite enough to be a devil. She 's
just what circumstances and her imagination
and other people happen to make her. A
child, that 's all.'

' You may think you know her,' Kingham
persisted obstinately, ' but you don't. How
can you, if you 've never been hunted by her ? '

' Bosh ! ' I said impatiently.

' I tell you she 's devilish,' he insisted.

'Then why on earth did you accept her invitation to lunch with such alacrity?'

'There are things that are unescapable,' he answered oracularly.

'I give you up,' I said, shrugging my shoulders. The man exasperated me. 'The best thing you can do,' I added, 'is to go to your devil and be damned as quickly as possible.'

'That's exactly where I am going,' he said. And as though I had reminded him of an appointment, Kingham looked at his watch. 'And by God,' he added, in a different voice, 'I shall have to take a taxi, if I 'm to get there in time.'

Kingham looked deeply put out; for he hated parting with money unnecessarily. He was tolerably well off now; but he still preserved the habits of prudence, almost of avarice, which he had acquired, painfully, in the days of his lower middle class boyhood and his poverty-stricken literary novitiate. He had asked Grace to dine with him in Soho; that had already cost him an effort. And now he was going to be compelled to take a taxi, so as to be in time to pay for the dinner. The thought of it made him suffer. And suffering for her sake, suffering a mean, unavowable pain for which he could not hope to get any sympathy, even his own, he found the ultimate cause of it, Grace, all the more devilish.

'Unescapable,' he repeated, still frowning, as he put on his hat to go. There was an expression positively of ferocity on his face. 'Unescapable.' He turned and left me.

'Poor Grace!' I was thinking, as I closed the front door and walked back to my study. It was just as unescapable for her as for Kingham. And I knew Kingham; my sympathies were all with Grace.

I was quite right, as it turned out, in according my sympathies as I did. For if any one ever needed, ever deserved sympathy, it was poor Grace, during those deplorable months of 1922. She fell in love with Kingham— fell in love, though it was the third time she had given herself, for the first, the very first time in her life, painfully, desperately, insanely. She had proposed to herself a repetition of her affair with Rodney. It was to be all charmingly perverse dalliances, with champagne and sandwiches and lightly tender conversation in the intervals; and exquisite little letters in the *dix-huitième* manner; and evening parties; and amusing escapades. That was what it had been with Rodney. He made this kind of love, it must be admitted, with real style; it was charming. Grace imagined that she would make it in just the same way with Rodney's successor. And so she might have, more or less, if the successor had been Levitski, or Masterman, or Gane. But the successor

123

was Kingham. The choice was fatal ; but the worst results of it might have been avoided if she had not loved him. Unloving, she might simply have left him when he made things too insupportable. But she did love him and, in love, she was utterly at his mercy.

Kingham had said that the thing was unescapable ; and if for him it was so, that was due to the need he perversely felt of giving himself over periodically to strong emotions, the need of being humiliated and humiliating, of suffering and making other people suffer. What he had always loved was the passion itself, not the women who were the cause or excuse of it. These occasional orgies of passion were necessary to him, just as the periodical drinking bout is necessary to the dipsomaniac. After a certain amount of indulgence, the need was satisfied and he felt quite free to detach himself from the lover who had been dear to him only as the stimulator of his emotions, not for her own sake. Kingham could satisfy his craving ; it was an appetite that could be quenched by indulgence. But Grace's desire was one of those desperate, hopeless desires that can only be assuaged by a kind of miracle. What she desired was nothing less than to unite herself wholly with another being, to know him through and through and to be made free of all his secrets. Only the all but miraculous meeting of two

equal loves, two equally confiding tempera-
ments can bring fulfilment to that longing.
There was no such meeting here.

Kingham made a habit of telling all his
acquaintances, sooner or later, what he thought
of them—which was invariably disagreeable.
He called this process a ' clearing of the atmosphere.' But in point of fact, it never cleared
anything ; it obscured and made turbid, it
created thunder in clear skies. Kingham
might not admit the fact; but this was, none
the less, precisely what he intended should
happen. Clear skies bored him ; he enjoyed
storms. But always, when he had succeeded
in provoking a storm, he expressed a genuine
astonishment at the inability of the world at
large to tolerate frankness, however sincere,
however manifestly for its own good. Hurt
by his brutally plain speaking, his old friends
were reproached for being hurt. Few of
Kingham's loves or friendships had long
survived the effects of his frankness. The
affair with Grace was one of the exceptions.

From the very beginning, Kingham had
found it necessary to ' clear the atmosphere.'
Even at their first meeting, in our house, he
was rather rude. Later on, he developed into
a kind of Timon of Athens. Her frivolity,
her voluptuary's philosophy of life, her heart-
lessness, her ' devilish concupiscence '—these
were the characteristics about which he told

her, with all the concentrated passion of which
he was capable, what he indignantly thought.

I met him again, at the Queen's Hall, on
the day after his dinner in Soho.

'I told her what I thought of her,' he let me
know.

'And what did she think about what you
thought?' I asked.

Kingham frowned. 'She seemed to be
rather pleased than otherwise,' he answered.
'That's the devilish strength of these women.
They simply glory in the things they ought
to be ashamed of. It makes them impervious
to anything decent. Impervious, and therefore utterly ruthless and unscrupulous.'

'How incorrigibly romantic you are!' I
mocked at him.

Told—and very mildly, after all—what I
thought of him, Kingham winced like a stung
horse. Other people's frankness hurt him
just as much as his hurt other people ; perhaps
more. The only difference was that he enjoyed being hurt.

'What nonsense!' he began indignantly.

His retort lasted as long as the interval and
was only drowned by the first blaring chords
of the *Meistersinger* overture. Bottled up
within compulsory silence, what were his
emotions? It amused me to speculate.
Various, emphatic, tirelessly unflagging and
working themselves up into ever more and

more clotted complications—were they not
the spiritual counterpart of this music to which
we were now listening ?   When the Wagner-
ian tumult was over, Kingham continued his
interrupted protest.

' She seemed to be rather pleased.'   That,
according to Kingham, had been Grace's re-
action to his home truths.   I felt sure, on
reflection, that he had observed her rightly.
For Grace still saw herself in terms of Rodneyism—as ' modern ' and ' eighteenth-century '
(curious how these terms have come to be
largely interchangeable) and what Rodney
imagined to be ' eternally feminine.'   Of
course she would be pleased at finding that
Kingham had accepted her at her own valuation
—and not only accepted her valuation but even
voluntarily outbidden it by adding devilishness
to the modernity, eighteenth-centuriness, and
eternal femininity which she had modestly—
too modestly, as she now perceived—attributed
to herself.   She took Kingham's denunciations as compliments and smiled with un-
affected pleasure when he talked to her of her
vampire's ruthlessness, when he reproached
her with her devilish concupiscence for the
shuddering souls as well as the less reluctant
flesh of her victims.   In Rodney's circle a
temperament was as much *de rigueur* as a train
and ostrich feathers at Court.   Grace saw
herself as a prodigy of temperament ;  but she

liked to have this vision of herself confirmed by outside testimony. Kingham's home truths convinced her that she had seen herself correctly. The more abusive Kingham became, the better pleased she was and the more she liked him. She felt that he was really taking her seriously as a frivolous woman, that he was appreciating her as she deserved. His appreciation heightened her confidence and, under the rain of his anathemas, she played her part with an easier grace, a more stylish perfection. The spectacle of Grace impertinently blossoming under what had been meant to blast exasperated Kingham. He abused her more violently ; and the greater his violence, the more serenely airy her eternal, modern, eighteenth-century femininity.

Underneath, meanwhile, and almost unconsciously, Grace was falling in love with him.

I have seen Kingham in his relations with many men and women. To none of them was he merely indifferent. Either they detested him—and I have never known a man who had more and bitterer enemies—or else they loved him. (Many of the lovers, I may add, turned subsequently into haters.) When I analyse my own feelings towards him, I am forced to the conclusion that I myself was in some manner in love with him. For why should I, who knew him so well and how insufferable he could be and, indeed, generally

was, why should I have put up with him, in
spite of everything ? And why should I
always have made such efforts to patch up all
our incessant quarrels ? Why shouldn't I
have allowed him to go to the devil, so far as
I was concerned, a dozen times ? or at least
thankfully accepted the estrangement which
followed our most violent squabble—the
squabble over poor loutish Herbert—and
allowed the separation to lengthen into per-
manency ? The only explanation is that, like
all those who did not loathe him, I was somehow in love with Kingham. He was in some
way important for me, deeply significant and
necessary. In his presence I felt that my being
expanded. There was suddenly, so to speak,
a high tide within me ; along dry, sand-silted,
desolate channels of my being life strongly,
sparklingly flowed. And Kingham was the
moon that drew it up across the desert.

All those whom we find sympathetic exercise,
in a greater or less degree, this moon-like influence upon us, drawing up the tides of life
till they cover what had been, in an antipathetic
environment, parched and dead. But there
are certain individuals who, by their proximity,
raise a higher tide, and in a vastly greater
number of souls, than the ordinary man or
woman. Kingham was one of these excep-
tional beings. To those who found him
sympathetic he was more sympathetic than

other and much more obviously amiable acquaintances. There was a glow, a vividness, a brilliance about the man. He could charm you even when he was saying things with which you disagreed, or doing things which you disapproved. Even his enemies admitted the existence and the power of this brilliant charm. Catherine, who was not exactly an enemy, but who profoundly disliked his way of life and habits of mind, had to confess that, whenever he wanted and took the trouble to do so, he could silence, for the moment at any rate, all her prejudices and compel her, so long as he was actually there, in the room with her, to like him. Grace started with no prejudices against him—no prejudices, beyond the opinion, inherited from Rodney, that the man was a savage ; and savages, after all, are more attractive than repellant. She was suggestible and easily swayed by stronger and more definite personalities than her own. It was not surprising that she should succumb to his charm to the extent of first liking the man and soon wildly loving him.

It was some little time, however, before Grace discovered that she loved him. In the first days of their intimacy, she was too busy playing the modern part to realize that she felt so un-Rodneyan an emotion. Love, the real insane thing, was out of harmony with the character she had assumed. It needed a

sudden, startling shock to make her understand what she felt for him, to make her, in
the same moment, forget to be ' modern ' and
' feminine ' in Rodney's sense of the terms,
and become—what ? I had meant to say
' herself.' But after all, can one be said to be
' oneself ' when one is being transfigured or
dolorously distorted by love ? In love, nobody
is himself ; or if you prefer, romantically, to
put it the other way round, nobody is really
himself when he is not in love. It comes to
very much the same thing. The difference
between Grace in love and Grace out of it
seemed all the wider, because it was the difference between a Rodneyan eternal female and a
woman, and a Kinghamized woman at that.
For even in love, Grace saw herself in the part
and saw herself, inevitably, in terms of her
lover. Her Rodneyisms disappeared and were
replaced by Kinghamisms. She saw herself
no longer as a modern young aristocrat, but as
the primevally ' passional ' incarnation (' passional ' was one of Kingham's too favourite
words) of her new lover's feminine ideal.

Their intimacy had lasted more than a
month before Grace discovered the true nature
of her feelings. Kingham's courtship had
been unremitting. Denunciations of her
devilishness had alternated with appeals to
her to become his mistress. Grace took the
denunciations as compliments and laughingly

replied to them at random with any nonsense that came into her head. These airy irrelevant retorts of hers, which Rodney would have applauded as the height of modern wit, seemed to Kingham the very height of diabolism.

'She's like Nero,' he said to me one day, 'fiddling over Rome.'

He was Rome—the centre of the universe—in flames. Grace, having kindled, watched him burn and, in the face of his destruction, talked nonsense.

What was more, she would not quench his conflagration. In spite of the 'devilish concupiscence,' which Kingham had attributed to her, she refused, during the first five or six weeks of their acquaintance, to become his mistress. She had captivated Kingham; that was sufficient to restore her self-confidence and that fantastic image of herself, as a successful, modern siren, which Rodney's desertion had temporarily shattered. To have tumbled into his arms at once might, perhaps, have been in the *dix-huitième* part; but a certain native modesty prevented Grace from being perfectly consistent.

Kingham regarded her refusal to capitulate immediately as yet another piece of devilishness; according to his theory, she was exercising an unnatural self-control merely in order to torment him. A perverse taste for cruelty was added to his list of accusations. Grace was charmed by this soft impeachment.

Kingham's attacks had seemed to her, so far, more amusing than painful, more complimentary than insulting. She was still protected by the armour of her indifference. The realization that she loved him was soon to strip her of that armour, and with every increase of that love, her naked spirit was to grow more tremulously sensitive to Kingham's assaults upon it.

The critical, the apocalyptic event took place in Kingham's rooms. It was a damp, hot afternoon of early summer. The sky was overcast when Grace arrived, and there was thunder in the air. She was wearing—the fact came out in her account to Catherine of the afternoon's events—she was wearing, for the first time, a brand new frock from Paris ; mouse-coloured, with two subtly harmonious, almost discordant, tones of red about the collar, and a repetition of the same colours at the cuffs and in a panel let into the skirt. Poiret, I think, was the inventor ; and it was very modern and rather eccentrically elegant. In a word, it was a dress created for Rodney's mistress.

Grace, who was very much aware of herself in her clothes, had felt the incongruity most painfully, afterwards. The more so, since, when she came in, she was feeling so happy about her dress. She was thinking what a success it was and how elegant, how original the people who saw her in the street must find her. And she was wondering what effect the dress would have on Kingham. She hoped, she thought that he would like it.

In his way, Kingham was nearly as observant in the matter of clothes as Rodney. True, he had not Rodney's almost professional eye for style and cut and smartness. Rodney was a great couturier *manqué*. The fashionable dressmaker was visible in every picture he painted ; he had mistaken his profession. Kingham's way of looking at clothes was different. His was the moralist's eye, not the couturier's. For him, clothes were symbols, the visible expressions of states of soul. Thus, Grace's slightly eccentric, very dashing elegance seemed to him the expressive symbol of her devilishness. He regarded her clothes as an efflorescence of her spirit. They were part of her, and she was directly and wholly responsible for them. It never seemed to strike him that tailors, dressmakers and advisory friends might share the responsibility. He took in Grace's frock at a glance.

'You've got a new dress on,' he said accusingly.

'Do you like it ?' she asked.

'No,' said Kingham.

'Why not ?'

'Why not ?' he repeated. 'Well, I suppose it's because the thing's so expressive of you, because it suits you so devilishly well.'

'I should have thought that would be a reason for liking it.'

'Oh, it would be, no doubt,' said Kingham, 'it would be, if I could just regard you as a spectacle, as something indifferent, to be looked at—that's all—like a picture. But you're not indifferent to me, and you know it and you deliberately torture me. How can I be expected to like what makes you seem more devilishly desirable and so increases my torture?'

He glared at her ferociously. It was with an effort that Grace kept her own gaze steady before those bright, dark, expressive eyes. He advanced towards her and laid his two hands on her shoulders.

'To-day,' he said, 'you're going to be my lover.'

Grace shook her head, smiling a capricious, eternally feminine smile.

'Yes, you arc.' His grip on her shoulders tightened.

'No, I'm not,' Grace answered. She drew in her breath rather sharply ; he was hurting her.

'I tell you, you are.'

They looked at one another, face close to face, enemies. Grace's heart violently beat.

'At one moment, I thought he was going to throttle me,' she told Catherine.

But she braved it out, and conquered.

135

Kingham withdrew his hands from her shoulders and turned away. He walked across to the other side of the room and, leaning against the wall in the embrasure of the window, looked out in silence at the grey sky.

Greatly relieved, Grace sat down on the divan. With a saucy and defiant movement that was, unfortunately, quite lost on Kingham's stubbornly presented back, she tucked up her feet under her. Opening her handbag, she took out her cigarette case, opened that in its turn, extracted a cigarette and lighted it—all very nonchalantly and deliberately. She was steadying her nerves to resist another attack—steadying her nerves and perhaps, at the same time, preparing to annoy him, when he should turn round, by the spectacle of her unconcernedness.

She had expected a repetition of the violences of a moment since, of the familiar denunciations of all the other days. She was not prepared to resist the new kind of attack which he now launched against her emotions. When at last—and she had more than half finished her cigarette before the long silence was broken —Kingham turned round and came towards her, she saw that he was weeping.

Kingham, as I have said, was no comedian. All that he professed to feel he felt, I am sure, genuinely. But he felt too easily and he was too fond of feeling. In situations where others

would have exercised a restraint upon themselves, Kingham gave free rein to his emotions,
or even actually roused and goaded them into
a more violent and more prolonged activity.
He needed no dervish tricks to work himself
up, no dancing, no howling and drumming,
no self-laceration. He could do the thing
inwardly, by intense concentration on the object
of his desire or hatred, on the cause of his pain
or pleasure. He brooded over his loves or
his grievances, making them seem more
significant than they really were ; he brooded,
conjuring up in his imagination appropriate
visions—of unpermitted raptures, when he
was suffering from the pangs of desire ; of
scenes of insult, humiliation, rage, when he
was angry with any one ; of his own miserable
self, when he desired to feel self-pity—himself,
pictured as unloved, in solitude, utterly
deserted, even dying. . . .

Long practice had made him an adept in the
art of working up his emotions, of keeping
himself uninterruptedly on the boil, so to
speak, over a long period of time. In the
course of these few brief weeks of his courtship, he had managed to convince himself that
the interest he took in Grace was the most
violent of passions and that he was suffering
excruciatingly from her refusal—her devilish,
her sadistic refusal—to be his mistress.
Painfully and profoundly, he was enjoying it.

The zest was still in the orgy ; he felt no sense of satiety.

These tears were the result of a sudden and overwhelming feeling of self-pity, which had succeeded his mood of violence. He had perceived, all at once, that his violence was futile ; it was absurd to suppose that he could shake or beat or throttle her into accepting him. He turned away in despair. He was alone, an outcast ; nobody cared for him ; he was expending his spirit in a waste of shame—his precious, beautiful spirit—and there was no saving himself, the madness was too strong. He was done for, absolutely done for.

Standing there, in the embrasure of the window, he had brooded over his miseries, until his sense of them became all of a sudden intolerable. The tears came into his eyes. He felt like a child, like a tired child who abandons himself, hopelessly, to misery.

All the animation went out of his face ; it became like the face of a dead man, frozen into a mask of quiet misery. Pale, ruddy-bearded, delicately featured, it was like the face of a dead or dying Christ in some agonizing Flemish picture.

It was this dead Christ's face that now turned back towards Grace Peddley. This dead Christ's face—and it had been the face of Lucifer, burning with life and passion, menacingly, dangerously beautiful, that had turned away from her.   The eyes, which had shone so brightly then, were almost shut, giving the face an appearance of blindness ; and between the half-closed lids there was a slow welling out of tears.

The first sight of this suffering face startled her into a kind of terror.   But the terror was succeeded almost at once by a great pity. That face, at once lifeless and suffering !   And those tears !   She had never seen a man shed tears before.   She was overwhelmed by pity— by pity and, at the thought that it was all her fault, by a passion of repentance and self-abasement, by a desire to make amends.   And at the same time she felt another and greater emotion, an emotion in which the pity and the repentance were included and from which they derived their strange intensity.   It was the feeling that, for her, Kingham was the only person in the world who in any way mattered.   It was love.

In silence he crossed the room, dropped down on his knees before the divan where Grace, her cigarette still smoking between her fingers, half sat, half reclined, frozen by astonishment into a statue of lolling modernity, and laying his head in her lap, silently sobbed.

The spell of Grace's immobility was broken. She bent forward over him, she caressed his hair.   The gesture recalled to her attention the half-smoked cigarette ; she threw it into the fire-place.   Her fingers touched his scalp, the nape of his neck, his ears, his averted cheek.

' My darling,' she whispered, ' my darling. You mustn't cry. It 's terrible when you cry.'

And she herself began to cry. For a long time they remained in the same position, Kingham kneeling, his face pressed against her knees, Grace bending over him, stroking his hair, both weeping.

Our thoughts and feelings are interdependent. It is only in language, not in fact, that they are separate and sharply differentiated. Some men are better mathematicians when they are in love than when they are out of it ; some are worse. But in either case the emotion of love conditions the working of the intellect. Still more powerfully does it affect the other emotions, such as pity, courage, shame, fear of ridicule, which it enhances or diminishes as the case may be. It may be laid down as a general rule that the feeling of one strong emotion predisposes us automatically to the feeling of other emotions, however apparently incongruous with the first. Thus joy may predispose to pity and shame to anger. Anger and grief may both dispose to sensual desire. Violent disputes often end in lovemaking ; and there are sometimes strange orgies over new-made graves, orgies, to the eye of the indifferent spectator, most unseemly, but which, as often as not, should be attributed less to a cynical lack of feeling than to its abundant presence. Grief creates a sense of loneliness, a desire in those who feel it to be comforted. At the same time, by throwing the whole personality into commotion, it renders the soul of the sufferer peculiarly susceptible to voluptuous influences and peculiarly unapt, in its state of disorganization, to exercise the customary self-restraints ; so that when the desired comforter appears, it sometimes happens (conditions of sex and age being propitious) that sympathy is transformed, not merely into love, but into desires demanding immediate satisfaction. Some such transformation took place now. Tears gave place to kisses less and less tearful, to caresses and embracements. There were languors and ecstatic silences.

' I love you, I love you,' Grace repeated, and was almost frightened by the vehemence of the new emotions, the intensity of the new and piercing sensations which she expressed in these old, blunted words. ' I love you.'

And Kingham kissed her and permitted himself, for the moment, to be happy without reserve or inward comment, without a touch of that anticipated afterthought which turns the present into history, even as it unrolls itself, and—criticizing, appraising, judging and condemning—takes all the zest out of immediacy. He was simply happy.

The time came for them to part.

' I must go,' said Grace, sighing.

But the Grace who went was a different woman from the Grace who had come, two hours before. It was a worshipping, adoring Grace, a Grace made humble by love, a Grace for whom being modern and a *grande dame* and eighteenth-century and intellectually fashionable had suddenly ceased to have the slightest importance. Adjusting her hair before the glass, she was struck by the incongruity, the garish out-of-placeness of her new frock. Her love for Kingham, she felt, was something vast and significant, something positively holy ; in the presence of that love, the new dress seemed a clown's livery worn in a church. Next day she wore an old, pre-Rodney dress—white muslin with black dots ; not at all showy, fashionable, or eccentric. Her soul had dressed itself, so to speak, to match.

But Kingham, who had had time in the intervening hours to poison the memory of yesterday's joy with every kind of venomous afterthought, to discover subtle and horrible explanations for actions that were obviously innocent and simple, received her as though she had changed neither her dress nor her spirit and were indeed the woman whose part she had been playing all these weeks.

' Well,' he said, as he opened the door to her, ' I see you 've come for more.'

Grace, who had expected to be received with

the gentle and beautiful tenderness which he had displayed on the previous day, was cruelly surprised by the brutality of his tone, the coldness and bitterness of his expression.

'More what?' she asked; and from brightly exultant her eyes became apprehensive in their expression, the smile with which she had so eagerly entered the room faded, as she halted in front of him. Anxiously she looked into his face. 'More what?'

Kingham laughed a loud, unpleasant, mirthless laugh, and pointed to the divan. Grace's devilish concupiscence—that was what he had been chiefly dwelling on since last he saw her.

For the first second Grace did not understand what he meant. This particular aspect of their love was so far from her mind, that it did not occur to her to imagine that it could be in Kingham's. Then all at once his meaning dawned upon her. The blood ran up into her cheeks.

'Kingham!' she protested. (Kingham was one of those men whom everybody, even his closest intimates, called by his surname. For the rest, he had only a pair of initials— J. G. I never knew what they stood for. John George, I should think. But it was quite irrelevant; he was always 'Kingham,' pure and simple.) 'Kingham! How can you say such things?'

'How can I?' he repeated mockingly.

'Why, by not keeping a fig-leaf over my mouth, which is where the truly respectable, who never talk about their vices, always keep it. Do what you like, but don't talk about it; that's respectability. But dear me,' he bantered on, 'I thought you were as much beyond respectability as you are beyond good and evil —or below, whichever the case may be.'

Grace, who had come in expecting a kiss and gentle words, walked slowly away from him across the room, sat down on the divan and began to cry.

A moment later Kingham was holding her in his arms and kissing away her tears. He spoke no word; the kisses became more passionate. At first, she averted her face from them. But in the end she abandoned herself. For a time she was happy. She forgot Kingham's cruel words, or if she remembered them, she remembered them as words spoken in a nightmare—by mistake, so to say, not on purpose, not seriously.

She had begun to feel almost perfectly reassured, when Kingham disengaged himself suddenly and roughly from her embrace, jumped up and began restlessly walking up and down the room, ruffling his hair as he went.

'What a horrible thing it is to have a vice!' he began. 'Something you carry about with you, but that isn't yourself. Something that's stronger than you are, that you want to resist

and conquer, but can't. A vice, a vice.' He
was enchanted by the word ; it became, for
the moment, the core of his universe. 'It's
horrible. We're possessed by devils, that's
what's wrong with us. We carry our private
devils about with us, our vices, and they're
too strong for us. They throw us down
and horribly triumph.' He shuddered dis-
gustedly. 'It's horrible to feel yourself being
murdered by your vice. The devil spiritually
murdering you, suffocating your soul with
warm soft flesh. My devil uses you as his instrument of murder ; your devil uses me. Our
vices conspire ; it's a conspiracy, a murder plot.'

By this time Grace was unhappier than she
had ever been in her life before. (And yet, if
Rodney had said the same thing, expressed a
little differently—in terms of compliments on
her 'temperament'—she would have been
delighted, two months ago.)

'But you know I love you, you *know*,' was
all that she could say. 'What makes you say
these things, when you know ? '

Kingham laughed. 'Oh, I know,' he
answered, 'I know, only too well. I know
what women like you mean by " love." '

'But I'm not a woman like . . .' Grace
hesitated ; 'like me' didn't sound quite
sensible, somehow. '. . . like that.'

'Not like yourself ? ' Kingham asked derisively.

'Not like what you think,' Grace insisted through the tangled confusion of words. 'Not silly, I mean ; not frivolous and all that. Not really.' All those months with Rodney seemed a dream ; and yet she had really lived through them. And there had really been champagne and sandwiches, and more than scientific conversations. . . . 'Not now, at any rate,' she added. 'Now I know you. It's different ; can't you understand. Utterly different. Because I love you, love you, love you, love you.'

Any one else would have allowed himself to be convinced, at any rate for the moment ; would have begged pardon, kissed and made friends. But, for Kingham, that would have been too easy, too emotionally flat. He stuck to his position.

'I know you do,' he answered, averting his gaze, as he spoke, from that pathetic, suffering face, from those wide-open grey eyes, perplexed and agonized, that looked up at him so appealingly, so abjectly even. 'So do I. Your devil loves me. My devil loves you.'

'But no,' Grace brokenly protested. 'But why ? . . .'

'Loves violently,' he went on in a loud voice, almost shouting, 'irresistibly.' And as he spoke the words he swung round and precipitated himself upon her with a kind of fury. 'Do you know what it is,' he went on, as he held her, struggling a little and reluctant in his arms, ' do you know what it is to love, not a person, not even their whole body, but just some part of it—insanely ? Do you know what it is when the vice-devil concentrates its whole desire on one point, focuses it inexorably until nothing else exists but the nape of a neck, or a pectoral muscle, a foot, a knee, a hand ? This hand, for example.' He took her hand and lifted it towards his face. ' And not even a whole hand,' he continued. ' Just the ball of a thumb, just that little cushion of flesh that 's marked off from the rest of the palm by the line of life ; just that soft, resilient, strong little cushion of flesh.'

He began to kiss the spot on Grace's hand.

' Don't, don't. You mustn't.' She tried to pull her hand away.

But Kingham held it fast. He went on kissing that soft, rounded swell of muscle at the base of her palm, insistently, again and again ; kissing and kissing. And sometimes he would take the flesh between his teeth and would bite, gently at first, then with a gradually increasing force, until the pain became almost unbearable and Grace cried out, when he would fall to kissing again, softly and tenderly, as though he were asking forgiveness, were trying to kiss the pain away. Grace ceased to struggle and abandoned her hand to him, to do with what he liked. And little by little this

insanely limited devil's love-making seemed
to evoke a special voluptuous sensibility in that
particular square inch of skin upon which it
was concentrated. Her whole capacity for
feeling pleasure seemed to focus itself at the
base of her left hand. Even the gradually
increasing pain, as his teeth closed more and
more tightly on her flesh, was pleasurable.
She abandoned herself ; but, at the same time,
she felt that there was something shameful
and even horrible about this pleasure. What
might have been simple and beautiful and
joyous had been turned into something painful,
complicated, ugly and obscure. Kingham
might congratulate himself on having produced a situation full of the most promising
emotional possibilities.

I have reconstructed these scenes at some
length because they were characteristic and
typical of the whole affair. In his search for
intense and painful emotions, Kingham displayed a perverse ingenuity ; he was never at
a loss for a pretext to complicate the simple
and distort the natural. His great resource
was always Grace's devilishness. Blind, as
only Kingham could be blind, to all evidence
to the contrary, he persisted in regarding Grace
as a frivolous vampire, a monster of heartless
vice. Her vampirishness and her vice were
the qualities which attracted him to her ; if he
could have been convinced that she was really

simple, innocent and childish, that her
' devilish concupiscence ' was in actual fact an
abject, unhappy adoration, he would have
ceased to take any interest in her. Pleading
meant as little to him as evidence. If Grace
protested too vigorously, Kingham would
bring up the affair with Rodney. What was
that but vice, plain and unvarnished ? Had
not she herself admitted that she didn't love
the man ? Miserably, despairingly, Grace
would confess in answer that she had certainly
been silly and frivolous and feather-headed,
but that now all that was done with. Everything was different, she was different, now.
Because she loved him. To which Kingham
would retort by expatiating with fiery eloquence
about the horrors of vice, until at last Grace
began to cry.

Grace's devilishness formed the staple and
chronic pretext for scenes. But Kingham
was inventive and there were plenty of other
excuses. Observant—for he was acutely observant, wherever he chose not to be blind—
Kingham had early realized the entirely vague
and accidental nature of all Grace's ideas,
convictions, principles, and opinions. He
perceived that what she thought about music,
for example, was only a distorted and fragmentary version of what I thought ; that her
opinions on art were Rodney's, muddled ; that
her philosophic and literary convictions were

like a parboiled lobster—' the fading sable and
the coming gules '—half Rodney's and half,
already, his own. And perceiving these
things, he mocked her for her intellectual
hypocrisy and snobbery. He found plenty of
opportunities for hurting and humiliating her.

On other occasions, he would reproach her
with untruthfulness and mean dissimulation,
because she did not frankly tell John Peddley
of her infidelity to him.

' I don't want to make him unnecessarily
miserable,' Grace protested.

Kingham laughed derisively. ' A lot you
care about anybody's happiness,' he said,
' particularly his ! The truth is that you want
to make the best of both worlds—be respectable and vicious at the same time. At all
costs, no frankness ! It 's a case of the mis-
placed fig-leaf, as usual.'

And then there was a terrible scene, a whole
series of terrible scenes, because Grace did not
want to have a child by him.

' Our only excuse,' he raged at her, ' the
only thing that might justify us—and you
won't hear of it. It 's to be vice for vice's
sake, is it ? The uncontaminated aesthetic
doctrine.'

At other times, becoming strangely solicitous
for the welfare of Grace's children, he reproached her with being a bad, neglectful
mother.

' And you know, it 's true,' she said to
Catherine, with remorseful conviction. ' It 's
quite true. I *do* neglect them.'

She invited Catherine to accompany her
and the two youngest to the Zoo, the very next
afternoon. Over the heads of little Pat and
Mittie, among the elephants and apes, the
bears and the screaming parrots, she talked to
Grace about her love and her unhappiness.
And every now and then Pat or Mittie would
interrupt with a question.

' Mummy, why do fish swim ? '

Or : ' How do you make tortoises ? '

' You know, you 're a great comfort,' said
Grace to Catherine, as they parted. ' I don't
know what I should do without you.'

The next time she came, she brought
Catherine a present ; not a powder-puff this
time, not gloves or ribbons, but a copy of
Dostoievsky's *Letters from the Underworld*.

' You must read it,' she insisted. ' You
absolutely must. It 's so damnably *true*.'

Grace's life during this period was one of
almost uninterrupted misery. I say ' almost
uninterrupted ' ; for there were occasions
when Kingham seemed to grow tired of violent
emotions, of suffering, and the infliction of
suffering ; moments when he was all tenderness and an irresistible charm. For these
brief spells of happiness, Grace was only too
pathetically grateful. Her love, which an

absolutely consistent ill-treatment might finally perhaps have crushed and eradicated, was revived by these occasional kindnesses into fresh outflowerings of a passionate adoration. Each time she hoped, she almost believed, that the happiness was going to be permanent. Bringing with her a few select aphorisms of Nietzsche, a pocket Leopardi, or the reproduction of one of Goya's *Desastres de la Guerra*, she would come and tell Catherine how happy she was, how radiantly, miraculously happy. Almost she believed that, this time, her happiness was going to last for ever. Almost ; but never quite. There was always a doubt, an unexpressed, secret, and agonizing fear. And always the doubt was duly justified, the fear was proved to be but too well founded. After two or three days' holiday from his emotional orgy—two or three days of calm and kindness —Kingham would appear before her, scowling, his face dark, his eyes angry and accusing. Grace looked at him and her heart would begin to beat with a painful irregularity and violence ; she felt suddenly almost sick with anxious anticipation. Sometimes he burst out at once. Sometimes—and that was much worse —he kept her in a state of miserable suspense, that might be prolonged for hours, even for days, sulking in a gloomy silence and refusing, when Grace asked him, to tell her what was the matter. If she ventured to approach him in one of these moods with a kiss or a soothing caress, he pushed her angrily away.

The excuses which he found for these renewals of tempest after calm were of the most various nature. One of the periods of happiness ended by his reproaching her with having been too tenderly amorous (too devilishly concupiscent) when he made love to her. On another occasion it was her crime to have remarked, two days before he chose actually to reproach her for it, that she liked the critical essays of Dryden. (' Such an intolerable piece of humbug and affectation,' he complained. ' Just because it 's the fashion to admire these stupid, boring classical writers. Mere hypocrisy, that 's what it is.' And so on.) Another time he was furious because she had insisted on taking a taxi all the way to Hampton Court. True, she had proposed from the first to pay for it. None the less, when the time came for paying, he had felt constrained in mere masculine decency to pull out his pocket-book. For one painful moment he had actually thought that she was going to accept his offer. He avenged himself for that moment of discomfort by accusing her of stupid and heartless extravagance.

' There 's something extraordinarily coarse,' he told her, ' something horribly thick-skinned and unfeeling about people who have been born and brought up with money. The idea

153

of spending a couple of pounds on a mere senseless caprice, when there are hundreds of thousands of people with no work, living precariously, or just not dying, on state charity ! The idea ! '

Grace, who had proposed the excursion because she thought that Hampton Court was the most romantic place in the world, and because it would be so wonderful to be two and lovers by the side of the Long Water, in the deep embrasures of the windows, before the old grey mirrors, before the triumphing Mantegnas—Grace was appalled that reality should have turned out so cruelly different from her anticipatory dreams. And meanwhile yet another moment of happiness had irrevocably passed.

It was not surprising that Grace should have come to look tired and rather ill. She was paler than in the past and perceptibly thinner. Rimmed with dark circles of fatigue, her eyes seemed to have grown larger and of a paler grey. Her face was still the face of a nice but rather ugly little girl—but of a little girl most horribly ill-treated, hopelessly and resignedly miserable.

Confronted by this perfect resignation to unhappiness, Catherine became impatient.

' Nobody 's got any business to be so resigned,' she said. ' Not nowadays, at any rate. We 've got beyond the Patient Griselda stage.'

154

But the trouble was that Grace hadn't got beyond it. She loved abjectly. When Catherine urged and implored her to break with Kingham, she only shook her head.

'But you 're unhappy,' Catherine insisted.

'There 's no need for you to tell me that,' said Grace, and the tears came into her eyes. 'Do you suppose I don't know it ?'

'Then why don't you leave him ?' asked Catherine. 'Why on earth don't you ?'

'Because I can't.' And after she had cried a little, she went on in a voice that was still unsteady and broken by an occasional sob : 'It 's as though there were a kind of devil in me, driving me on against my will. A kind of dark devil.' She had begun to think in terms of Kingham even about herself. The case seemed hopeless.

We went abroad that summer, to the seaside, in Italy. In the lee of that great limestone mountain which rises suddenly, like the mountain of Paradise, out of the Pomptine marshes and the blue plains of the Mediterranean, we bathed and basked and were filled with the virtue of the life-giving sun. It was here, on the flanks of this mountain, that the enchantress Circe had her palace. Circeus Mons, Monte Circeo—the magic of her name has lingered, through Roman days, to the present. In coves at the mountain's foot stand the ruins of imperial villas, and walking

under its western precipices you come upon
the ghost of a Roman seaport, with the fish-
ponds of Lucullus close at hand, like bright
eyes looking upwards out of the plain. At
dawn, before the sun has filled all space with
the quivering gauzes of heat and the colourless
brightness of excessive light, at dawn and
again at evening, when the air once more grows
limpid and colour and distant form are re-born,
a mountain shape appears, far off, across the
blue gulf of Terracina, a mountain shape
and a plume of white unwavering smoke :
Vesuvius. And once, climbing before sun-
rise to the crest of our Circean hill, we saw
them both—Vesuvius to the southward, across
the pale sea and northwards, beyond the green
marshes, beyond the brown and ilex-dark
Alban hills, the great symbolical dome of the
world, St. Peter's, glittering above the mists
of the horizon.

We stayed at Monte Circeo for upwards of
two months, time enough to become brown
as Indians and to have forgotten, or at least to
have become utterly careless of, the world
outside. We saw no newspapers ; dis-
couraged all correspondents by never answering their letters, which we hardly even took
the trouble to read ; lived, in a word, the life
of savages in the sun, at the edge of a tepid sea.
All our friends and relations might have died,
England been overwhelmed by war, pestilence

and famine, all books, pictures, music destroyed irretrievably out of the world—at Monte Circeo we should not have cared a pin.

But the time came at last when it was necessary to return to London and make a little money. We loaded our bodies with unaccustomed garments, crammed our feet— our feet that had for so long enjoyed the liberty of sandals—into their imprisoning shoes, took the omnibus to Terracina and climbed into the train.

'Well,' I said, when we had managed at last to squeeze ourselves into the two vacant places which the extraordinary exuberance of a party of Neapolitans had painfully restricted, 'we 're going back to civilization.'

Catherine sighed and looked out of the window at the enchantress's mountain beckoning across the plain. 'One might be excused,' she said, 'for making a little mistake and thinking it was hell we were going back to.'

It was a dreadful journey. The compartment was crowded and the Neapolitans fabulously large, the weather hot, the tunnels frequent, and the smoke peculiarly black and poisonous. And with the physical there came a host of mental discomforts. How much money would there be in the bank when we got home? What bills would be awaiting us? Should I be able to get my book on Mozart finished by Christmas, as I had promised?

In what state should I find my invalid sister?
Would it be necessary to pay a visit to the
dentist? What should we do to placate all
the people to whom we had never written?
Wedged between the Neapolitans, I wondered.
And looking at Catherine, I could see by the
expression on her face that she was similarly
preoccupied. We were like Adam and Eve
when the gates of the garden closed behind
them.

At Genoa the Neapolitans got out and were
replaced by passengers of more ordinary
volume. The pressure in the compartment
was somewhat relaxed. We were able to
secure a couple of contiguous places. Conversation became possible.

'I've been so much wondering,' said
Catherine, when at last we were able to talk,
'what's been happening all this time to poor
little Grace. You know, I really *ought* to
have written to her.' And she looked at me
with an expression in which consciousness of
guilt was mingled with reproach.

'After all,' I said, responding to her expression rather than to her words, 'it wasn't my
fault if you were too lazy to write. Was it?'

'Yes, it was,' Catherine answered. 'Just
as much yours as mine. You ought to have
reminded me to write, you ought to have
insisted. Instead of which you set the
example and encouraged my laziness.'

I shrugged my shoulders. ' One can't argue with women.'

' Because they 're almost always in the right,' said Catherine. ' But that isn't the point. Poor Grace is the point. What 's happened to her, do you suppose ? And that dreadful Kingham—what has he been up to ? I wish I 'd written.'

At Monte Circeo, it is true, we had often spoken of Grace and Kingham. But there, in the annihilating sunshine, among the enormous and, for northern eyes, the almost unreal beauties of that mythological landscape, they had seemed as remote and as unimportant as everything and everybody else in our other life. Grace suffered. We knew it, no doubt, theoretically ; but not, so to speak, practically —not personally, not with sympathetic realization. In the sun it had been hardly possible to realize anything beyond our own well-being. Expose a northern body to the sun and the soul within it seems to evaporate. The inrush from the source of physical life drives out the life of the spirit. The body must become inured to light and life before the soul can condense again into active existence. When we had talked of Grace at Monte Circeo, we had been a pair of almost soulless bodies in the sun. Our clothes, our shoes, the hideous discomfort of the train gave us back our souls. We talked of Grace now with rediscovered sympathy, speculating rather anxiously on her fate.

' I feel that in some way we 're almost responsible for her,' said Catherine. ' Oh, I wish I 'd written to her ! And why didn't she write to me ? '

I propounded a comforting theory. ' She probably hasn't been with Kingham at all,' I suggested. ' She 's gone abroad as usual with Peddley and the children. We shall probably find that the whole thing has died down by the time we get home.'

' I wonder,' said Catherine.

We were destined to discover the truth, or at least some portion of it, sooner than we had expected. The first person I saw as I stepped out of the train at Modane was John Peddley.

He was standing on the platform some ten or fifteen yards away, scanning, with eyes that sharply turned this way and that, the faces of the passengers descending from the express. His glances were searching, quick, decisive. He might have been a detective posted there on the frontier to intercept the escape of a criminal. No crook, you felt, no gentleman cracksman, however astute, could hope to sneak or swagger past those all-seeing hunter's eyes. It was that thought, the realization that the thing was hopeless, that made me check my first impulse, which was to flee—out of the station, anywhere—to hide—in the luggage-

van, the lavatory, under a seat. No, the game
was obviously up. There was no possible
escape. Sooner or later, whatever I might do
now, I should have to present myself at the
custom-house ; he would catch me there,
infallibly. And the train was scheduled to
wait for two and a half hours.

' We 're in for it,' I whispered to Catherine,
as I helped her down on to the platform. She
followed the direction of my glance and saw
our waiting danger.

' Heaven help us,' she ejaculated with an
unaccustomed piety ; then added in another
tone : ' But perhaps that means that Grace
is here. I shall go and ask him.'

' Better not,' I implored, still cherishing a
foolish hope that we might somehow slip past
him unobserved. ' Better not.'

But in that instant, Peddley turned round
and saw us. His large, brown, handsome
face beamed with sudden pleasure ; he positively ran to meet us.

Those two and a half hours in John Peddley's
company at Modane confirmed for me a rather
curious fact, of which, hitherto, I had been
only vaguely and inarticulately aware : the
fact that one may be deeply and sympathetically interested in the feelings of individuals
whose thoughts and opinions—all the products,
in a word, of their intellects—are utterly indifferent, even wearisome and repulsive. We

read the Autobiography of Alfieri, the Journals of Benjamin Robert Haydon, and read them with a passionate interest. But Alfieri's tragedies, but Haydon's historical pictures, all the things which, for the men themselves, constituted their claim on the world's attention, have simply ceased to exist, so far as we are concerned. Intellectually and artistically, these men were more than half dead. But emotionally they lived.

*Mutatis mutandis*, it was the same with John Peddley. I had known him, till now, only as a relater of facts, an expounder of theories—as an intellect, in short ; one of the most appallingly uninteresting intellects ever created. I had known him only in his public capacity, so to speak, as the tireless lecturer of club smoking-rooms and dinner-tables. I had never had a glimpse of him in private life. It was not to be wondered at ; for, as I have said before, at ordinary times and when things were running smoothly, Peddley had no private life more complicated than the private life of his body. His feelings towards the majority of his fellow-beings were the simple emotions of the huntsman : pleasure when he had caught his victim and could talk him to death ; pain and a certain slight resentment when the prey escaped him. Towards his wife he felt the desires of a healthy man in early middle life, coupled with a real but rather

162

unimaginative, habit-born affection. It was an affection which took itself and its object, Grace, altogether too much for granted. In his own way, Peddley loved his wife, and it never occurred to him to doubt that she felt in the same way towards him ; it seemed to him the natural inevitable thing, like having children and being fond of them, having a house and servants and coming home in the evening from the office to find dinner awaiting one. So inevitable, that it was quite unnecessary to talk or even to think about it ; natural to the point of being taken publicly for granted, like the possession of a bank balance.

I had thought it impossible that Peddley should ever develop a private life ; but I had been wrong. I had not foreseen the possibility of his receiving a shock violent enough to shake him out of complacency into self-questioning, a shock of sufficient strength to shiver the comfortable edifice of his daily, taken-for-granted life. That shock he had now received. It was a new and unfamiliar Peddley who now came running towards us.

' I 'm so glad, I 'm so particularly glad to see you,' he said, as he approached us. ' Quite extraordinarily glad, you know.'

I have never had my hand so warmly shaken as it was then. Nor had Catherine, as I could see by the way she winced, as she abandoned her fingers to his crushing cordiality.

163

' You 're the very man I particularly wanted
to see,' he went on, turning back to me.   He
stooped and picked up a couple of our suit-
cases.   ' Let 's make a dash for the douane,'
he said.   ' And then, when we 've got those
wretched formalities well over, we can have a
bit of a talk.'

We followed him.   Looking at Catherine,
I made a grimace.   The prospect of that bit
of a talk appalled me.   Catherine gave me an
answering look, then quickened her pace so
as to come up with the energetically hurrying
Peddley.

' Is Grace with you here ? ' she asked.

Peddley halted, a suit-case in each hand.
' Well,' he said, slowly and hesitatingly, as
though it were possible to have metaphysical
doubts about the correct answer to this question, ' well, as a matter of fact, she isn't.   Not
really.'   He might have been discussing the
problem of the Real Presence.

As if reluctant to speak about the matter
any further, he turned away and hurried on
towards the custom-house, leaving Catherine's
next question—' Shall we find her in London
when we get back ? '—without an answer.

The bit of a talk, when it came, was very
different from what I had gloomily anticipated.

' Do you think your wife would mind,'
Peddley whispered to me, when the douanier
had done with us and we were making our

way towards the station restaurant, ' if I had a few words with you alone ? '

I answered that I was sure she wouldn't, and said a word to Catherine, who replied, to me by a quick significant look, and to both of us together by a laughing dismissal.

' Go away and talk your stupid business if you want to,' she said. ' I shall begin my lunch.'

We walked out on to the platform. It had begun to rain, violently, as it only rains among the mountains. The water beat on the vaulted glass roof of the station, filling all the space beneath with a dull, continuous roar ; we walked as though within an enormous drum, touched by the innumerable fingers of the rain. Through the open arches at either end of the station the shapes of mountains were dimly visible through veils of white, wind-driven water.

We walked up and down for a minute or two without saying a word. Never, in my presence at any rate, had Peddley preserved so long a silence. Divining what embarrassments kept him in this unnatural state of speechlessness, I felt sorry for the man. In the end, after a couple of turns up and down the platform, he made an effort, cleared his throat and diffidently began in a small voice that was quite unlike that loud, self-assured, trombone-like voice in which he told one about the Swiss banking system.

' What I wanted to talk to you about,' he said, ' was Grace.'

The face he turned towards me as he spoke was full of a puzzled misery. That commonplacely handsome mask was strangely puckered and lined. Under lifted eyebrows, his eyes regarded me, questioningly, helplessly, unhappily.

I nodded and said nothing ; it seemed the best way of encouraging him to proceed.

' The fact is,' he went on, turning away from me and looking at the ground, ' the fact is . . .' But it was a long time before he could make up his mind to tell me what the fact was.

Knowing so very well what the fact was, I could have laughed aloud, if pity had not been stronger in me than mockery, when he wound up with the pathetically euphemistic understatement : ' The fact is that Grace . . . well, I believe she doesn't love me. Not in the way she did. In fact I know it.'

' How do you know it ? ' I asked, after a little pause, hoping that he might have heard of the affair only through idle gossip, which I could proceed to deny.

' She told me,' he answered, and my hope disappeared.

' Ah.'

So Kingham had had his way, I reflected. He had bullied her into telling Peddley the quite unnecessary truth, just for the sake of making the situation a little more difficult and painful than it need have been.

' I 'd noticed for some time,' Peddley went on, after a silence, ' that she 'd been different.'

Even Peddley could be perspicacious after the event. And besides, the signs of her waning love had been sufficiently obvious and decisive. Peddley might have no sympathetic imagination ; but at any rate he had desires and knew when they were satisfied and when they weren't. He hinted at explanatory details.

' But I never imagined,' he concluded—'how could I imagine ?—that it was because there was somebody else. How could I ? ' he repeated in a tone of ingenuous despair. You saw very clearly that it was, indeed, quite impossible for him to have imagined such a thing.

' Quite,' I said, affirming comfortingly I do not know exactly what proposition. ' Quite.'

' Well then, one day,' he pursued, ' one day just before we had arranged to come out here into the mountains, as usual, she suddenly came and blurted it all out—quite suddenly, you know, without warning. It was dreadful. Dreadful.'

There was another pause.

' That fellow called Kingham,' he went on, breaking the silence, ' you know him ? he 's a friend of yours, isn't he ? '

I nodded.

167

'Very able man, of course,' said Peddley, trying to be impartial and give the devil his due. 'But, I must say, the only times I met him I found him rather unsympathetic.' (I pictured the scene : Peddley embarking on the law relating to insurance companies or, thoughtfully remembering that the chap was literary, on pianolas or modern art or the Einstein theory. And for his part, Kingham firmly and in all likelihood very rudely refusing to be made a victim of.) 'A bit too eccentric for my taste.'

'Queer,' I confirmed, 'certainly. Perhaps a little mad sometimes.'

Peddley nodded. 'Well,' he said slowly, 'it was Kingham.'

I said nothing. Perhaps I ought to have 'registered amazement,' as they say in the world of the cinema ; amazement, horror, indignation—above all amazement. But I am a poor comedian. I made no grimaces, uttered no cries. In silence we walked slowly along the platform. The rain drummed on the roof overhead ; through the archway at the end of the station the all but invisible ghosts of mountains loomed up behind white veils. We walked from Italy towards France and back again from France towards Italy.

'Who could have imagined it ?' said Peddley at last.

'Anybody,' I might, of course, have

168

answered. 'Anybody who had a little imagination and who knew Grace ; above all, who knew you.' But I held my tongue. For though there is something peculiarly ludicrous about the spectacle of a self-satisfaction suddenly punctured, it is shallow and unimaginative only to laugh at it. For the puncturing of self-satisfaction gives rise to a pain that can be quite as acute as that which is due to the nobler tragedies. Hurt vanity and exploded complacency may be comic as a spectacle, from the outside ; but to those who feel the pain of them, who regard them from within, they are very far from ludicrous. The feelings and opinions of the actor, even in the morally lowest dramas, deserve as much consideration as the spectator's. Peddley's astonishment that his wife could have preferred another man to himself was doubtless, from my point of view, a laughable exhibition. But the humiliating realization had genuinely hurt him ; the astonishment had been mixed with a real pain. Merely to have mocked would have been a denial, in favour of the spectator, of the actor's rights. Moreover, the pain which Peddley felt was not exclusively the product of an injured complacency. With the low and ludicrous were mingled other, more reputable emotions. His next words deprived me of whatever desire I might have had to laugh.

'What am I to do ?' Peddley went on,

after another long pause, and looked at me again more miserably and bewilderedly than ever. ' What *am* I to do ? '

' Well,' I said cautiously, not knowing what to advise him, ' it surely depends how you feel about it all—about Grace in particular.'

' How I feel about her ? ' he repeated. ' Well,' he hesitated, embarrassed, ' I 'm fond of her, of course. Very fond of her.' He paused ; then, with a great effort, throwing down barriers which years of complacent silence, years of insensitive taking for granted had built up round the subject, he went on : ' I love her.'

The utterance of that decisive word seemed to make things easier for Peddley. It was as though an obstruction had been removed ; the stream of confidences began to flow more easily and copiously.

' You know,' he went on, ' I don't think I had quite realized how much I did love her till now. That 's what makes it all so specially dreadful—the thought that I ought to have loved her more, or at least more consciously when I had the opportunity, when she loved me ; the thought that if I had, I shouldn't, probably, be here now all alone, without her.' He averted his face and was silent, while we walked half the length of the platform. ' I think of her all the time, you know,' he continued. ' I think how happy we used to be together and I wonder if we shall ever be happy again, as we were, or if it 's all over, all finished.' There was another pause. 'And then,' he said, 'I think of her there in England, with that man, being happy with him, happier perhaps than she ever was with me ; for perhaps she never really did love me, not like that.' He shook his head. 'Oh, it 's dreadful, you know, it 's dreadful. I try to get these thoughts out of my head, but I can't. I walk in the hills till I 'm dead-beat ; I try to distract myself by talking to people who come through on the trains. But it 's no good. I can't keep these thoughts away.'

I might have assured him, of course, that Grace was without doubt infinitely less happy with Kingham than she had ever been with him. But I doubted whether the consolation would really be very efficacious.

'Perhaps it isn't really serious,' I suggested, feebly. 'Perhaps it won't last. She 'll come to her senses one of these days.'

Peddley sighed. 'That 's what I always hope, of course. I was angry at first, when she told me that she wasn't coming abroad and that she meant to stay with that man in England. I told her that she could go to the devil, so far as I was concerned. I told her that she 'd only hear from me through my solicitor. But what was the good of that ? I don't want her to go to the devil ; I want her to be with me. I 'm not angry any more, only miserable. I 've even swallowed my pride. What 's the good of being proud and not going back on your decisions, if it makes you unhappy ? I 've written and told her that I want her to come back, that I 'll be happy and grateful if she does.'

' And what has she answered ? ' I asked.

' Nothing,' said Peddley.

I imagined Peddley's poor conventional letter, full of those worn phrases that make their appearance with such a mournful regularity in all the letters that are read in the divorce courts, or before coroners' juries, when people have thrown themselves under trains for unrequited love. Miserable, cold, inadequate words ! A solicitor, he had often dictated them, no doubt, to clients who desired to have their plea for the restitution of conjugal rights succinctly and decorously set down in black and white, for the benefit of the judge who was, in due course, to give it legal force. Old, blunted phrases, into which only the sympathy of the reader has power to instil a certain temporary life—he had had to write them unprofessionally this time, for himself.

Grace, I guessed, would have shown the letter to Kingham. I imagined the derisive ferocity of his comments. A judicious analysis of its style can reduce almost any love-letter to emptiness and absurdity. Kingham would have made that analysis with gusto and with a devilish skill. By his mockery he had doubtless shamed Grace out of her first spontaneous feelings ; she had left the letter unanswered. But the feelings, I did not doubt, still lingered beneath the surface of her mind ; pity for John Peddley and remorse for what she had done. And Kingham, I felt sure, would find some ingenious method for first encouraging, then deriding these emotions. That would agreeably complicate their relations, would render her love for him a source of even greater pain to her than ever.

Peddley broke the rain-loud silence and the train of my speculations by saying : ' And if it is serious, if she goes on refusing to answer when I write—what then ? '

' Ah, but that won't happen,' I said, speaking with a conviction born of my knowledge of Kingham's character. Sooner or later he would do something that would make it impossible for even the most abject of lovers to put up with him. ' You can be sure it won't.'

' I only wish I could,' said Peddley dubiously : he did not know Kingham, only Grace —and very imperfectly at that. ' I can't guess what she means to do. It was all so unexpected—from Grace. I never imagined . . .' For the first time he had begun to realize his ignorance of the woman to whom he was married. The consciousness of this ignorance was one of the elements of his distress. 'But if it is serious,' he went on, after a pause, obstinately insisting on contemplating the worst of possibilities, 'what am I to do? Let her go, like that, without a struggle? Set her free to go and be permanently and respectably happy with that man?' (At the vision he thus conjured up of a domesticated Kingham, I inwardly smiled.) 'That would be fairest to her, I suppose. But why should I be unfair to myself?'

Under the fingers of the drumming rain, in the presence of the ghostly, rain-blurred mountains, we prolonged the vain discussion. In the end I persuaded him to do nothing for the time being. To wait and see what the next days or weeks or months would bring. It was the only possible policy.

When we returned to the station restaurant, Peddley was considerably more cheerful than when we had left it. I had offered no very effectual consolation, invented no magical solution of his problems; but the mere fact that he had been able to talk and that I had been ordinarily sympathetic had been a relief and a comfort to him. He was positively rubbing his hands as he sat down beside Catherine.

'Well, Mrs. Wilkes,' he said in that professionally hearty tone which clergymen, doctors, lawyers, and all those whose business

it is to talk frequently and copiously with
people they do not know, so easily acquire,
' well, Mrs. Wilkes, I 'm afraid we 've shame-
fully neglected you. I 'm afraid you 'll never
forgive me for having carried off your husband
in this disgraceful way.' And so on.

After a little, he abandoned this vein of
graceful courtesy for more serious conversation.
' I met a most interesting man at this station
a few days ago,' he began. ' A Greek. Theotocopulos was his name. A very remarkable
man. He told me a number of most illuminating things about King Constantine and the
present economic situation in Greece. He
assured me, for one thing, that . . .' And
the information about King Constantine and
the economic situation in Hellas came pouring
out. In Mr. Theotocopulos, it was evident,
John Peddley had found a kindred soul.
When Greek meets Greek then comes, in this
case, an exchange of anecdotes about the
deposed sovereigns of eastern Europe—in a
word, the tug of bores. From private, Peddley had returned to public life. We were
thankful when it was time to continue our
journey.

Kingham lived on the second floor of a
once handsome and genteel eighteenth-century
house, which presented its façade of blackened
brick to a decayed residential street, leading
northward from Theobald's Road towards the

easternmost of the Bloomsbury Squares. It was a slummy street in which, since the war, a colony of poor but 'artistic' people from another class had settled. In the windows, curtains of dirty muslin alternated with orange curtains, scarlet curtains, curtains in large bright-coloured checks. It was not hard to know where respectable slumminess ended and gay Bohemianism began.

The front door of number twenty-three was permanently open. I entered and addressed myself to the stairs. Reaching the second landing, I was surprised to find the door of Kingham's rooms ajar. I pushed it open and walked in.

'Kingham,' I called, 'Kingham!'

There was no answer. I stepped across the dark little vestibule and tapped at the door of the main sitting-room.

'Kingham!' I called again more loudly.

I did not want to intrude indiscreetly upon some scene of domestic happiness or, more probably, considering the relations existing between Grace and Kingham, of domestic strife.

'Kingham!'

The silence remained unbroken. I walked in. The room was empty. Still calling discreetly as I went, I looked into the second sitting-room, the kitchen, the bedroom. A pair of suit-cases were standing, ready packed,

just inside the bedroom door.   Where could
they be going ?   I wondered, hoped I should
see them before they went.   Meanwhile, I
visited even the bathroom and the larder ; the
little flat was quite empty of life.   They must
have gone out, leaving the front door open
behind them as they went.   If preoccupation
and absence of mind be signs of love, why then,
I reflected, things must be going fairly well.

It was twenty to six on my watch.   I decided
to wait for their return.   If they were not back
within the hour, I would leave a note, asking
them to come to see us, and go.

The two small and monstrously lofty sitting-
rooms in Kingham's flat had once been a single
room of nobly classical proportions.   A lath-
and-plaster partition separated one room from
the other, dividing into two unsymmetrical
parts the gracefully moulded design which
had adorned the ceiling of the original room.
A single tall sash window, having no pro-
portionable relation to the wall in which it
found itself accidentally placed, illuminated
either room—the larger inadequately, the
smaller almost to excess.   It was in the smaller
and lighter of the two sitting-rooms that
Kingham kept his books and his writing-table.
I entered it, looked round the shelves, and
having selected two or three miscellaneous
volumes, drew a chair up to the window and
settled down to read.

'I have no patience,' I read (and it was a volume of Kingham's own writings that I had opened), 'I have no patience with those silly prophets and Utopia-mongers who offer us prospects of uninterrupted happiness. I have no patience with them. Are they too stupid even to realize their own stupidity? Can't they see that if happiness were uninterrupted and well-being universal, these things would cease to be happiness and well-being and become merely boredom and daily bread, daily business, *Daily Mail*? Can't they understand that, if everything in the world were pea-green, we shouldn't know what pea-green was? " Asses, apes and dogs ! " (Milton too, thank God for Milton ! didn't suffer fools gladly. Satan—portrait of the artist.) Asses, apes and dogs. Are they too stupid to see that, in order to know happiness and virtue, men must also know misery and sin? The Utopia I offer is a world where happiness and unhappiness are more intense, where they more rapidly and violently alternate than here, with us. A world where men and women endowed with more than our modern sensitiveness, more than our acute and multifarious modern consciousness, shall know the unbridled pleasures, the cruelties and dangers of the ancient world, with all the scruples and remorses of Christianity, all its ecstasies, all its appalling fears. That is the Utopia I offer you—not a sterilized

nursing home, with Swedish drill before breakfast, vegetarian cookery, classical music on the
radio, chaste mixed sun-baths, and rational free
love between aseptic sheets.   Asses, apes and
dogs ! '

One thing at least, I reflected, as I turned
the pages of the book in search of other attractive paragraphs, one thing at least could be
said in Kingham's favour ;  he was no mere
academic theorist.   Kingham practised what
he preached.   He had defined Utopia, he was
doing his best to realize it—in Grace's company.

'Vows of chastity,' the words caught my
eye and I read on, ' vows of chastity are ordinarily taken in that cold season, full of disgusts
and remorses, which follows after excess.   The
taker of the oath believes the vow to be an
unbreakable chain about his flesh.   But he is
wrong ;  the vow is no chain, only a hempen
strand.   When the blood is cold, it holds fast.
But when, with the natural rebirth of appetite,
the blood turns to flame, that fire burns through
the hemp—the tindery hemp which the binder
had thought to be a rope of steel—burns it, and
the flesh breaks loose.   With renewed satiety
come coldness, disgust, remorse, more acute
this time than before, and with them a repetition of the Stygian vows.   And so on, round
and round, like the days of the week, like
summer and winter.   Futile, you say, no

doubt ; weak-minded. But I don't agree with you. Nothing that intensifies and quickens life is futile. These vows, these remorses and the deep-rooted feeling from which they spring—the feeling that the pleasure of the senses is somehow evil— sharpen this pleasure to the finest of points, multiply the emotions to which it gives rise by creating, parallel with the body's delight, an anguish and tragedy of the mind.'

I had read them before, these abbreviated essays or expanded maxims (I do not know how to name them ; Kingham himself had labelled them merely as ' Notions ') ; had read them more than once and always enjoyed their violence, their queerness, their rather terrifying sincerity. But this time, it seemed to me, I read them with greater understanding than in the past. My knowledge of King- ham's relations with Grace illuminated them for me ; and they, in their turn, threw light on Kingham and his relations with Grace. For instance, there was that sentence about love : ' All love is in the nature of a vengeance ; the man revenges himself on the woman who has caught and humiliated him ; the woman revenges herself on the man who has broken down her reserves and reluctances, who has dared to convert her from an individual into a mere member and mother of the species.' It seemed particularly significant to me, now. I remember noticing, too, certain words about the sin against the Holy Ghost. ' Only those who know the Holy Ghost are tempted to sin against him—indeed, can sin against him. One cannot waste a talent unless one first possesses it. One cannot do what is wrong, or stupid, or futile, unless one first knows what is right, what is reasonable, what is worth doing. Temptation begins with knowledge and grows as knowledge grows. A man knows that he has a soul to save and that it is a precious soul ; it is for that very reason that he passes his time in such a way that it must infallibly be damned. You, reader,' the paragraph characteristically concluded, ' you who have no soul to save, will probably fail to understand what I am talking about.'

I was considering these words in the light of the recent increases of my knowledge of Kingham, when I was suddenly interrupted in the midst of my meditations by the voice of Kingham himself.

' It 's no good,' it was saying. ' Can't you understand ? ' The voice sounded all at once much louder, as the door of the larger sitting-room opened to admit the speaker and his companion. Their footsteps resounded on the uncarpeted boards. ' Why will you go on like this ? ' He spoke wearily, like one who is tired of being importuned and desires only to be left in peace. ' Why will you ? '

' Because I love you.'  Grace's voice was low and dulled.   It seemed to express a kind of obstinate misery.

' Oh, I know, I know,' said Kingham with an impatience that was muted by fatigue.   He sighed noisily.  ' If you only knew how sick I was of all this unnecessary higgling and arguing ! '  The tone was almost pathetic ; it seemed to demand that one should condole with the speaker, that one should do one's best to spare him pain.   One might have imagined, from the tone of his voice, that Kingham was the persecuted victim of a relentless Grace. And it was thus indeed that he now saw himself, if, as I guessed, he had reached that inevitable closing phase of all his passions— the phase of emotional satiety.   He had drunk his fill of strong feeling ;  the bout was over, for this time, the zest had gone out of the orgy. He wanted only to live quietly, soberly.   And here was Grace, importuning him to continue the orgy.  An orgy in cold blood—ugh ! For a man sobered by complete satiety, the idea was disgustful, a thought to shudder at. No wonder he spoke thus plaintively.  ' I tell you,' he went on, ' it 's settled.  Definitely. Once and for all.'

' You mean it ?   You mean definitely that you 're going ? '

' Definitely,' said Kingham.

' Then I mean what I 've said,' the miserable,

dully obstinate voice replied. 'Definitely. I shall kill myself if you go.'

My first impulse, when I heard Kingham's voice, had been—goodness knows why—to hide myself. A sudden sense of guilt, a schoolboy's terror of being caught, entirely possessed me. My heart beating, I jumped up and looked about me for some place of concealment. Then, after a second or two, my reason reasserted itself. I remembered that I was not a schoolboy in danger of being caught and caned ; that, after all, I had been waiting here in order to ask Kingham and Grace to dinner ; and that, so far from hiding myself, I ought immediately to make my presence known to them. Meanwhile, sentence had succeeded sentence in their muffled altercation. I realized that they were involved in some terrible, mortal quarrel ; and realizing, I hesitated to interrupt them. One feels shy of breaking in on an exhibition of strong and intimate emotion. To intrude oneself, clothed and armoured in one's daily indifference, upon naked and quivering souls is an insult, almost, one feels, an indecency. This was evidently no vulgar squabble, which could be allayed by a little tact, a beaming face and a tepid douche of platitude. Perhaps it was even so serious, so agonizing that it ought to be put an end to at all costs. I wondered. Ought I to intervene ? Knowing Kingham, I was afraid that my intervention might only make things worse. So far from shaming him into peace, it would in all probability have the effect of rousing all his latent violences. To continue an intimately emotional scene in the presence of a third party is a kind of indecency. Kingham, I reflected, would probably be only too glad to enhance and complicate the painfulness of the scene by introducing into it this element of spiritual outrage. I stood hesitating, wondering what I ought to do. Go in to them and run the risk of making things worse? Or stay where I was, at the alternative risk of being discovered, half an hour hence, and having to explain my most inexplicable presence? I was still hesitating when, from the other room, the muffled, obstinate voice of Grace pronounced those words :

'I shall kill myself if you go.'

'No, you won't,' said Kingham. 'I assure you, you won't.' The weariness of his tone was tinged with a certain ironic mockery.

I imagined the excruciations which might result if I gave Kingham an audience to such a drama, and decided not to intervene—not yet, at any rate. I tiptoed across the room and sat down where it would be impossible for me to be seen through the open door.

'I've played that little farce myself,' Kingham went on. 'Oh, dozens of times. Yes, and really persuaded myself at the moment that it was the genuinely tragic article.' Even without my intervention, his mockery was becoming brutal enough.

' I shall kill myself,' Grace repeated, softly and stubbornly.

' But as you see,' Kingham pursued, ' I 'm still alive.' A new vivacity had come into his weary voice. ' Still alive and perfectly intact. The cyanide of potassium always turned out to be almond icing : and however carefully I aimed at my cerebellum, I never managed to score anything but a miss.' He laughed at his own jest.

' Why will you talk in that way ? ' Grace asked, with a weary patience. ' That stupid, cruel way ? '

' I may talk,' said Kingham, ' but it 's you who act. You 've destroyed me, you 've poisoned me : you 're a poison in my blood. And you complain because I talk ! '

He paused, as if expecting an answer : but Grace said nothing. She had said all that there was for her to say so often, she had said ' I love you,' and had had the words so constantly and malevolently misunderstood, that it seemed to her, no doubt, a waste of breath to answer him.

' I suppose it 's distressing to lose a victim,' Kingham went on in the same ironic tone. ' But you can't really expect me to believe that it 's so distressing that you 've got to kill

yourself. Come, come, my dear Grace. That's
a bit thick.'

'I don't expect you to believe anything,'
Grace replied. 'I just say what I mean and
leave it at that. I'm tired.' I could hear by
the creaking of the springs that she had thrown
herself down on the divan. There was a silence.

'So am I,' said Kingham, breaking it at last.
'Mortally tired.' All the energy had gone
out of his voice ; it was once more blank
and lifeless. There was another creaking of
springs ; he had evidently sat down beside her
on the divan. 'Look here,' he said, ' for God's
sake let's be reasonable.' From Kingham,
the appeal was particularly cogent ; I could
not help smiling. 'I'm sorry I spoke like
that just now. It was silly ; it was bad-
tempered. And you know the way one word
begets another ; one's carried away. I didn't
mean to hurt you. Let's talk calmly. What's
the point of making an unnecessary fuss ?
The thing's inevitable, fatal. A bad business,
perhaps ; but let's try to make the best of it,
not the worst.'

I listened in astonishment, while Kingham
wearily unwound a string of such platitudes.
Wearily, wearily ; he seemed to be boring
himself to death with his own words. Oh, to
have done with it, to get away, to be free, never
again to set eyes on her ! I imagined his
thoughts, his desires.

There are moments in every amorous intimacy, when such thoughts occur to one or other of the lovers, when love has turned to weariness and disgust, and the only desire is a desire for solitude. Most lovers overcome this temporary weariness by simply not permitting their minds to dwell on it. Feelings and desires to which no attention is paid soon die of inanition ; for the attention of the conscious mind is their food and fuel. In due course love reasserts itself and the moment of weariness is forgotten. To Kingham, however, Kingham who gave his whole attention to every emotion or wish that brushed against his consciousness, the slightest velleity of weariness became profoundly significant. Nor was there, in his case, any real enduring love for the object of his thoughtfully fostered disgust, any strong and steady affection capable of overcoming what should have been only a temporary weariness. He loved because he felt the need of violent emotion. Grace was a means to an end, not an end in herself. The end—satisfaction of his craving for emotional excitement—had been attained ; the means had therefore ceased to possess the slightest value for him. Grace would have been merely indifferent to him, if she had shown herself in this crisis as emotionally cold as he felt himself. But their feelings did not synchronize. Grace was not weary ; she loved him, on the contrary, more passionately than ever. Her importunate warmth had conspired with his own habit of introspection to turn weariness and emotional neutrality into positive disgust and even hatred. He was making an effort, however, not to show these violent feelings ; moreover he was tired—too tired to want to give them their adequate expression. He would have liked to slip away quietly, without any fuss. Wearily, wearily, he uttered his sedative phrases. He might have been a curate giving Grace a heart-to-heart chat about Life.

'We must be sensible,' he said. And : 'There are other things besides love.' He even talked about self-control and the consolations of work. It lasted a long time.

Suddenly Grace interrupted him. 'Stop !' she cried in a startlingly loud voice. 'For heaven's sake stop ! How can you be so dishonest and stupid ?'

'I'm not,' Kingham answered, sullenly. 'I was simply saying . . .'

'You were simply saying that you're sick of me,' said Grace, taking up his words. 'Simply saying it in a slimy, stupid, dishonest way. That you're sick to death of me and that you wish to goodness I'd go away and leave you in peace. Oh, I will, I will. You needn't worry.' She uttered a kind of laugh.

There was a long silence.

'Why don't you go ?' said Grace at last.

Her voice was muffled, as though she were lying with her face buried in a cushion.

'Well,' said Kingham awkwardly. 'Perhaps it might be best.' He must have been feeling the beginnings of a sense of enormous relief, a joy which it would have been indecent to display, but which was bubbling only just beneath the surface. 'Good-bye, then, Grace,' he said, in a tone that was almost cheerful. 'Let's part friends.'

Grace's laughter was muffled by the cushion. Then she must have sat up; for her voice, when she spoke a second later, was clear and unmuted.

'Kiss me,' she said peremptorily. 'I want you to kiss me, just once more.'

There was a silence.

'Not like that,' Grace's voice came almost angrily. 'Kiss me really, really, as though you still loved me.'

Kingham must have tried to obey her; anything for a quiet life and a prompt release. There was another silence.

'No, no.' The anger in Grace's voice had turned to despair. 'Go away, go, go. Do I disgust you so that you can't even kiss me?'

'But, my dear Grace . . .' he protested.

'Go, go, go.'

'Very well, then,' said Kingham in a dignified and slightly offended tone. But inwardly, what joy! Liberty, liberty! The key had

189

turned in the lock, the prison door was opening.
' If you want me to, I will.' I heard him
getting up from the divan. ' I 'll write to you
when I get to Munich,' he said.

I heard him walking to the door, along the
passage to the bedroom, where, I suppose, he
picked up·his suit-cases, back along the passage
to the outer door of the apartment. The latch
clicked, the door squeaked on its hinges as it
swung open, squeaked as it closed ; there was
an echoing bang.

I got up from my chair and cautiously
peeped round the edge of the doorway into the
other room. Grace was lying on the divan in
precisely the position I had imagined, quite
still, her face buried in a cushion. I stood
there watching her for perhaps half a minute,
wondering what I should say to her. Everything would sound inadequate, I reflected.
Therefore, perhaps, the most inadequate of all
possible words, the most perfectly banal,
trivial and commonplace, would be the best
in the circumstances.

I was pondering thus when suddenly that
death-still body stirred into action. Grace
lifted her face from the pillow, listened for a
second, intently, then with a series of swift
motions, she turned on her side, raised herself
to a sitting position, dropped her feet to the
ground and, springing up, hastened across the
room towards the door. Instinctively, I with-

drew into concealment. I heard her cross the passage, heard the click and squeak of the front door as it opened. Then her voice, a strange, inhuman, strangled voice, called ' Kingham ! ' and again, after a listening silence that seemed portentously long, ' Kingham ! ' There was no answer.

After another silence, the door closed. Grace's footsteps approached once more, crossed the room, came to a halt. I peeped out from my ambush. She was standing by the window, her forehead pressed against the glass, looking out—no, looking down, rather. Two storeys, three, if you counted the area that opened like a deep grave at the foot of the wall beneath the window—was she calculating the height ? What were her thoughts ?

All at once, she straightened herself up, stretched out her hands and began to raise the sash. I walked into the room towards her.

At the sound of my footsteps, she turned and looked at me—but looked with the disquietingly blank, unrecognizing eyes and expressionless face of one who is blind. It seemed as though her mind were too completely preoccupied with its huge and dreadful idea to be able to focus itself at once on the trivialities of life.

' Dear Grace,' I said, ' I 've been looking for you. Catherine sent me to ask you to come and have dinner with us.'

She continued to look at me blankly.    After
a second or two, the significance of my words
seemed to reach her ; it was as though she
were far away, listening to sounds that laboured
slowly across the intervening gulfs of space.
When at last she had heard my words—heard
them with her distant mind—she shook her
head and her lips made the movement of
saying ' No.'

I took her arm and led her away from the
window.    ' But you must,' I said.

My voice seemed to come to her more
quickly this time.    It was only a moment after
I had finished speaking that she again shook
her head.

' You must,' I repeated.    ' I heard everything, you know.    I shall make you come with
me.'

' You heard ? ' she repeated, staring at me.

I nodded, but did not speak.    Picking up
her small, close-fitting, casque-shaped hat from
where it was lying on the floor, near the divan,
I handed it to her.    She turned with an
automatic movement towards the dim, grey-
glassed Venetian mirror that hung above the
fireplace and adjusted it to her head : a wisp
of hair straggled over her temple ; tidily, she
tucked it away.

' Now, let 's go,' I said, and led her away,
out of the flat, down the dark stairs, into the
street.

Walking towards Holborn in search of a taxi, I made futile conversation. I talked, I remember, about the merits of omnibuses as opposed to undergrounds, about second-hand bookshops, and about cats. Grace said nothing. She walked at my side, as though she were walking in her sleep.

Looking at that frozen, unhappy face—the face of a child who has suffered more than can be borne—I was filled with a pity that was almost remorse. I felt that it was somehow my fault ; that it was heartless and insensitive of me not to be as unhappy as she was. I felt, as I have often felt in the presence of the sick, the miserably and hopelessly poor, that I owed her an apology. I felt that I ought to beg her pardon for being happily married, healthy, tolerably prosperous, content with my life. Has one a right to be happy in the presence of the unfortunate, to exult in life before those who desire to die ? Has one a right ?

' The population of cats in London,' I said, ' must be very nearly as large as the population of human beings.'

' I should think so,' Grace whispered, after a sufficient time had elapsed for her to hear, across the gulfs that separated her mind from mine, what I had said. She spoke with a great effort ; her voice was scarcely audible.

' Literally millions,' I pursued.

And then, fortunately, I caught sight of a

taxi. Driving home to Kensington, I talked to her of our Italian holiday. I did not think it necessary, however, to tell her of our meeting with Peddley at Modane.

Arrived, I told Catherine in two words what had happened and, handing Grace over to her care, took refuge in my work-room. I felt, I must confess, profoundly and selfishly thankful to be back there, alone, with my books and my piano. It was the kind of thankfulness one feels, motoring out of town for the week-end, to escape from dark and sordid slums to a comfortable, cool-gardened country house, where one can forget that there exist other human beings beside oneself and one's amusing, cultivated friends, and that ninety-nine out of every hundred of them are doomed to misery. I sat down at the piano and began to play the Arietta of Beethoven's Op. 111.

I played it very badly, for more than half my mind was preoccupied with something other than the music. I was wondering what would become of Grace now. Without Rodney, without Kingham, what would she do? What would she be? The question propounded itself insistently.

And then, all at once, the page of printed music before my eyes gave me the oracular reply. *Da capo.* The hieroglyph sent me back to the beginning of my passage. *Da capo.* After all, it was obvious. *Da capo.*

John Peddley, the children, the house, the blank existence of one who does not know how to live unassisted. Then another musical critic, a second me—introduction to the second theme. Then the second theme, *scherzando*; another Rodney. Or *molto agitato*, the equivalent of Kingham. And then, inevitably, when the agitation had agitated itself to the climax of silence, *da capo* again to Peddley, the house, the children, the blankness of her unassisted life.

The miracle of the Arietta floated out from under my fingers. Ah, if only the music of our destinies could be like this !

# HALF-HOLIDAY

## I

I⟨T⟩ was Saturday afternoon and fine. In the hazy spring sunlight London was beautiful, like a city of the imagination. The lights were golden, the shadows blue and violet. Incorrigibly hopeful, the sooty trees in the Park were breaking into leaf ; and the new green was unbelievably fresh and light and aerial, as though the tiny leaves had been cut out of the central emerald stripe of a rainbow. The miracle, to all who walked in the Park that afternoon, was manifest. What had been dead now lived ; soot was budding into rainbow green. Yes, it was manifest. And, moreover, those who perceived this thaumaturgical change from death to life were themselves changed. There was something contagious about the vernal miracle. Loving more, the loitering couples under the trees were happier—or much more acutely miserable. Stout men took off their hats, and while the sun kissed their bald heads, made good resolutions—about whisky, about the pretty typist at the office, about early rising. Accosted by spring-intoxicated boys, young girls consented, in the teeth of all their upbringing and their alarm, to go for walks. Middle-aged gentlemen, strolling homewards through the Park, suddenly felt their crusted, business-grimy hearts burgeoning, like these trees, with kindness and generosity. They thought of their wives, thought of them with a sudden gush of affection, in spite of twenty years of marriage. ' Must stop on the way back,' they said to themselves, ' and buy the missus a little present.' What should it be ? A box of candied fruits ? She liked candied fruits. Or a pot of azaleas ? Or . . . And then they remembered that it was Saturday afternoon. The shops would all be shut. And probably, they thought, sighing, the missus's heart would also be shut ; for the missus had not walked under the budding trees. Such is life, they reflected, looking sadly at the boats on the glittering Serpentine, at the playing children, at the lovers sitting, hand in hand, on the green grass. Such is life ; when the heart is open, the shops are generally shut. But they resolved nevertheless to try, in future, to control their tempers.

On Peter Brett, as on every one else who came within their range of influence, this bright spring sunlight and the new-budded trees profoundly worked. They made him feel, all at once, more lonely, more heart-broken than he had ever felt before. By contrast with the brightness around him, his soul seemed darker. The trees had broken into leaf ; but he remained dead. The lovers

walked in couples ; he walked alone. In
spite of the spring, in spite of the sunshine, in
spite of the fact that to-day was Saturday and
that to-morrow would be Sunday—or rather
because of all these things which should have
made him happy and which did make other
people happy—he loitered through the miracle
of Hyde Park feeling deeply miserable.

As usual, he turned for comfort to his
imagination. For example, a lovely young
creature would slip on a loose stone just in front
of him and twist her ankle. Grown larger than
life and handsomer, Peter would rush forward
to administer first aid. He would take her in
a taxi (for which he had money to pay) to her
home—in Grosvenor Square. She turned out
to be a peer's daughter. They loved each
other. . . .

Or else he rescued a child that had fallen
into the Round Pond and so earned the eternal
gratitude, and more than the gratitude, of its
rich young widowed mother. Yes, widowed ;
Peter always definitely specified her widow-
hood. His intentions were strictly honourable.
He was still very young and had been well
brought up.

Or else there was no preliminary accident.
He just saw a young girl sitting on a bench by
herself, looking very lonely and sad. Boldly,
yet courteously, he approached, he took off
his hat, he smiled. ' I can see that you 're

lonely,' he said ; and he spoke elegantly and
with ease, without a trace of his Lancashire
accent, without so much as a hint of that
dreadful stammer which, in real life, made
speech such a torment to him.  ' I can see that
you 're lonely.  So am I.  May I sit down
beside you ? '  She smiled, and he sat down.
And then he told her that he was an orphan
and that all he had was a married sister who
lived in Rochdale.  And she said, ' I 'm an
orphan too.'  And that was a great bond
between them.  And they told one another
how miserable they were.  And she began to
cry.  And then he said, ' Don't cry.  You 've
got me.'  And at that she cheered up a little.
And then they went to the pictures together.
And finally, he supposed, they got married.
But that part of the story was a little dim.

But of course, as a matter of fact, no acci-
dents ever did happen and he never had the
courage to tell any one how lonely he was ;
and his stammer was something awful ; and
he was small, he wore spectacles, and nearly
always had pimples on his face ; and his dark
grey suit was growing very shabby and rather
short in the sleeves ; and his boots, though
carefully blacked, looked just as cheap as they
really were.

It was the boots which killed his imaginings
this afternoon.  Walking with downcast eyes,
pensively, he was trying to decide what he

should say to the peer's lovely young daughter
in the taxi on the way to Grosvenor Square,
when he suddenly became aware of his alter-
nately striding boots, blackly obtruding themselves through the transparent phantoms of
his inner life. How ugly they were ! And
how sadly unlike those elegant and sumptu-
ously shining boots which encase the feet of
the rich ! They had been ugly enough when
they were new ; age had rendered them positively repulsive. No boot-trees had corrected
the effects of walking, and the uppers, just
above the toe-caps, were deeply and hideously
wrinkled. Through the polish he could see
a network of innumerable little cracks in the
parched and shoddy leather. On the outer
side of the left boot the toe-cap had come un-
stitched and had been coarsely sewn up again ;
the scar was only too visible. Worn by much
lacing and unlacing, the eyeholes had lost
their black enamel and revealed themselves
obtrusively in their brassy nakedness.

Oh, they were horrible, his boots ; they
were disgusting ! But they'd have to last
him a long time yet. Peter began to re-make
the calculations he had so often and often made
before. If he spent three-halfpence less every
day on his lunch ; if, during the fine weather,
he were to walk to the office every morning
instead of taking the bus. . . . But however
carefully and however often he made his

calculations, twenty-seven and sixpence a week
always remained twenty-seven and six.   Boots
were dear ;  and when he had saved up enough
to buy a new pair, there was still the question
of his suit.   And, to make matters worse, it
was spring ;  the leaves were coming out, the
sun shone, and among the amorous couples
he walked alone.   Reality was too much for
him to-day ;  he could not escape.   The boots
pursued him whenever he tried to flee, and
dragged him back to the contemplation of his
misery.

II

The two young women turned out of the
crowded walk along the edge of the Serpentine,
and struck uphill by a smaller path in the
direction of Watts's statue.   Peter followed
them.   An exquisite perfume lingered in the
air behind them.   He breathed it greedily and
his heart began to beat with unaccustomed
violence.   They seemed to him marvellous
and hardly human beings.   They were all that
was lovely and unattainable.   He had met
them walking down there, by the Serpentine,
had been overwhelmed by that glimpse of a
luxurious and arrogant beauty, had turned
immediately and followed them.   Why ?   He
hardly knew himself.   Merely in order that
he might be near them ; and perhaps with the
fantastic, irrepressible hope that something

201

might happen, some miracle, that should project him into their lives.

Greedily he sniffed their delicate perfume ; with a kind of desperation, as though his life depended on it, he looked at them, he studied them.   Both were tall.   One of them wore a grey cloth coat, trimmed with dark grey fur. The other's coat was all of fur ; a dozen or two of ruddily golden foxes had been killed in order that she might be warm among the chilly shadows of this spring afternoon.   One of them wore grey and the other buff-coloured stockings.   One walked on grey kid, the other on serpent's leather.   Their hats were small and close-fitting.   A small black French bull-dog accompanied them, running now at their heels, now in front of them.   The dog's collar was trimmed with brindled wolf's fur that stuck out like a ruff round its black head.

Peter walked so close behind them that, when they were out of the crowd, he could hear snatches of their talk.   One had a cooing voice ; the other spoke rather huskily.

' Such a divine man,' the husky voice was saying, ' such a really divine man ! '

' So Elizabeth told me,' said the cooing one.

' Such a perfect party, too,' Husky went on. ' He kept us laughing the whole evening. Everybody got rather buffy, too.   When it was time to go, I said I 'd walk and trust to luck to find a taxi on the way.   Whereupon

he invited me to come and look for a taxi in his
heart.   He said there were so many there, and
all of them disengaged.'

They both laughed.   The chatter of a party
of children who had come up from behind
and were passing at this moment prevented
Peter from hearing what was said next.   Inwardly he cursed the children.   Beastly little
devils—they were making him lose his revelation.   And what a revelation !   Of how
strange, unfamiliar and gaudy a life !   Peter's
dreams had always been idyllic and pastoral.
Even with the peer's daughter he meant to
live in the country, quietly and domestically.
The world in which there are perfect parties
where everybody gets rather buffy and divine
men invite young goddesses to look for taxis
in their hearts was utterly unknown to him.
He had had a glimpse of it now ; it fascinated
him by its exotic and tropical strangeness.
His whole ambition was now to enter this
gorgeous world, to involve himself, somehow
and at all costs, in the lives of these young
goddesses.   Suppose, now, they were both
simultaneously to trip over that projecting root
and twist their ankles.   Suppose . . .   But
they both stepped over it in safety.   And then,
all at once, he saw a hope—in the bulldog.

The dog had left the path to sniff at the base
of an elm tree growing a few yards away on the
right.   It had sniffed, it had growled, it had

left a challenging souvenir of its visit and was
now indignantly kicking up earth and twigs
with its hinder paws against the tree, when a
yellow Irish terrier trotted up and began in its
turn to sniff, first at the tree, then at the bulldog.
The bulldog stopped its scrabbling in the dirt
and sniffed at the terrier.  Cautiously, the two
beasts walked round one another, sniffing and
growling as they went.  Peter watched them
for a moment with a vague and languid curiosity.  His mind was elsewhere ; he hardly
saw the two dogs.  Then, in an illuminating
flash, it occurred to him that they might begin to fight.  If they fought, he was a made
man.  He would rush in and separate them,
heroically.  He might even be bitten.  But
that didn't matter.  Indeed, it would be all
the better.  A bite would be another claim on
the goddesses' gratitude.  Ardently, he hoped
that the dogs would fight.  The awful thing
would be if the goddesses or the owners of the
yellow terrier were to notice and interfere
before the fight could begin.  ' Oh God,' he
fervently prayed, ' don't let them call the dogs
away from each other now.  But let the dogs
fight.  For Jesus Christ's sake.  Amen.'
Peter had been piously brought up.

The children had passed.  The voices of
the goddesses once more became audible.

' . . . Such a fearful bore,' the cooing one
was saying.  ' I can never move a step without

finding him there. And nothing penetrates his hide. I 've told him that I hate Jews, that I think he 's ugly and stupid and tactless and impertinent and boring. But it doesn't seem to make the slightest difference.'

' You should make him useful, at any rate,' said Husky.

' Oh, I do,' affirmed Coo.

' Well, that 's something.'

' Something,' Coo admitted. ' But not much.'

There was a pause. 'Oh, God,' prayed Peter, ' don't let them see.'

' If only,' began Coo meditatively, ' if only men would understand that . . .' A fearful noise of growling and barking violently interrupted her. The two young women turned in the direction from which the sound came.

' Pongo ! ' they shouted in chorus, anxiously and commandingly. And again, more urgently, ' Pongo ! '

But their cries were unavailing. Pongo and the yellow terrier were already fighting too furiously to pay any attention.

' Pongo !   Pongo ! '

And, ' Benny ! ' the little girl and her stout nurse to whom the yellow terrier belonged as unavailingly shouted. ' Benny, come here ! '

The moment had come, the passionately anticipated, the richly pregnant moment. Exultantly, Peter threw himself on the dogs.

' Get away, you brute,' he shouted, kicking the Irish terrier.  For the terrier was the enemy, the French bulldog—*their* French bulldog— the friend whom he had come, like one of the Olympian gods in the Iliad, to assist.  ' Get away ! '  In his excitement, he forgot that he had a stammer.  The letter G was always a difficult one for him ; but he managed on this occasion to shout ' Get away ' without a trace of hesitation.  He grabbed at the dogs by their stumpy tails, by the scruffs of their necks, and tried to drag them apart.  From time to time he kicked the yellow terrier.  But it was the bulldog which bit him.  Stupider even than Ajax, the bulldog had failed to under- stand that the immortal was fighting on his side.  But Peter felt no resentment and, in the heat of the moment, hardly any pain.  The blood came oozing out of a row of jagged holes in his left hand.

' Ooh ! '  cried Coo, as though it were her hand that had been bitten.

' Be careful,' anxiously admonished Husky. ' Be careful.'

The sound of their voices nerved him to further efforts.  He kicked and he tugged still harder ; and at last, for a fraction of a second, he managed to part the angry beasts. For a fraction of a second neither dog had any portion of the other's anatomy in his mouth. Peter seized the opportunity, and catching the

French bulldog by the loose skin at the back of his neck, he lifted him, still furiously snapping, growling and struggling, into the air. The yellow terrier stood in front of him, barking and every now and then leaping up in a frantic effort to snap the dangling black paws of his enemy. But Peter, with the gesture of Perseus raising on high the severed head of the Gorgon, lifted the writhing Pongo out of danger to the highest stretch of his arm. The yellow dog he kept off with his foot ; and the nurse and the little girl, who had by this time somewhat recovered their presence of mind, approached the furious animal from behind and succeeded at last in hooking the leash to his collar. His four rigidly planted paws skidding over the grass, the yellow terrier was dragged away by main force, still barking, though feebly—for he was being half strangled by his efforts to escape. Suspended six feet above the ground by the leathery black scruff of his neck, Pongo vainly writhed.

Peter turned and approached the goddesses. Husky had narrow eyes and a sad mouth ; it was a thin, tragic-looking face. Coo was rounder, pinker and whiter, bluer-eyed. Peter looked from one to the other and could not decide which was the more beautiful.

He lowered the writhing Pongo. ' Here 's your dog,' was what he wanted to say. But the loveliness of these radiant creatures sud-

denly brought back all his self-consciousness
and with his self-consciousness his stammer.
'Here's your . . .' he began ; but could
not bring out the dog. D, for Peter, was
always a difficult letter.

For all common words beginning with a
difficult letter Peter had a number of easier
synonyms in readiness. Thus, he always
called cats ' pussies,' not out of any affectation
of childishness, but because p was more pro-
nounceable than the impossible c. Coal he
had to render in the vaguer form of ' fuel.'
Dirt, with him, was always ' muck.' In the
discovery of synonyms he had become almost
as ingenious as those Anglo-Saxon poets who,
using alliteration instead of rhyme, were
compelled, in their efforts to make (shall we
say) the sea begin with the same letter as its
waves or its billows, to call it the ' whale-road '
or the ' bath of the swans.' But Peter, who
could not permit himself the full poetic licence
of his Saxon ancestors, was reduced sometimes
to spelling the most difficult words to which
there happened to be no convenient and
prosaic equivalent. Thus, he was never quite
sure whether he should call a cup a mug or a
c, u, p. And since ' ovum ' seemed to be the
only synonym for egg, he was always reduced
to talking of e, g, g's.

At the present moment, it was the miserable
little word ' dog ' that was holding him up.

Peter had several synonyms for dog. P being
a slightly easier letter than d, he could, when
not too nervous, say 'pup.' Or if the p's
weren't coming easily, he could call the animal,
rather facetiously and mock-heroically, a
'hound.' But the presence of the two goddesses was so unnerving, that Peter found it as
hopelessly impossible to pronounce a p or an h
as a d. He hesitated painfully, trying to bring
out in turn, first dog, then pup, then hound.
His face became very red. He was in an agony.

'Here's your whelp,' he managed to say
at last. The word, he was conscious, was a
little too Shakespearean for ordinary conversation. But it was the only one which came.

'Thank you most awfully,' said Coo.

'You were splendid, really splendid,' said
Husky. 'But I'm afraid you're hurt.'

'Oh, it's n-nothing,' Peter declared. And
twisting his handkerchief round the bitten
hand, he thrust it into his pocket.

Coo, meanwhile, had fastened the end of
her leash to Pongo's collar. 'You can put
him down now,' she said.

Peter did as he was told. The little black
dog immediately bounded forward in the
direction of his reluctantly retreating enemy.
He came to the end of his tether with a jerk
that brought him up on to his hind legs and
kept him, barking, in the position of a rampant
lion on a coat of arms.

' But are you sure it 's nothing ? ' Husky insisted. ' Let me look at it.'

Obediently, Peter pulled off the handkerchief and held out his hand. It seemed to him that all was happening as he had hoped. Then he noticed with horror that the nails were dirty. If only, if only he had thought of washing before he went out ! What would they think of him ? Blushing, he tried to withdraw his hand. But Husky held it.

' Wait,' she said. And then added : ' It 's a nasty bite.'

' Horrid,' affirmed Coo, who had also bent over it. ' I 'm so awfully sorry that my stupid dog should have . . .'

' You ought to go straight to a chemist,' said Husky, interrupting her, ' and get him to disinfect it and tie it up.'

She lifted her eyes from his hand and looked into his face.

' A chemist,' echoed Coo, and also looked up.

Peter looked from one to the other, dazzled equally by the wide-open blue eyes and the narrowed, secret eyes of green. He smiled at them vaguely and vaguely shook his head. Unobtrusively he wrapped up his hand in his handkerchief and thrust it away, out of sight.

' It 's n-nothing,' he said.

' But you must,' insisted Husky.

' You must,' cried Coo.

' N-nothing,' he repeated. He didn't want

to go to a chemist. He wanted to stay with the goddesses.

Coo turned to Husky. ' Qu'est-ce qu'on donne à ce petit bonhomme ? ' she asked, speaking very quickly and in a low voice.

Husky shrugged her shoulders and made a little grimace suggestive of uncertainty. ' Il serait offensé, peut-être,' she suggested.

' Tu crois ? '

Husky stole a rapid glance at the subject of their discussion, taking him in critically from his cheap felt hat to his cheap boots, from his pale spotty face to his rather dirty hands, from his steel-framed spectacles to his leather watch-guard. Peter saw that she was looking at him and smiled at her with shy, vague rapture. How beautiful she was ! He wondered what they had been whispering about together. Perhaps they were debating whether they should ask him to tea. And no sooner had the idea occurred to him than he was sure of it. Miraculously, things were happening just as they happened in his dreams. He wondered if he would have the face to tell them—this first time—that they could look for taxis in his heart.

Husky turned back to her companion. Once more she shrugged her shoulders. ' Vraiment, je ne sais pas,' she whispered.

' Si on lui donnait une livre ? ' suggested Coo.

Husky nodded. ' Comme tu voudras.'

And while the other turned away to fumble unobtrusively in her purse, she addressed herself to Peter.

'You were awfully brave,' she said, smiling.

Peter could only shake his head, blush and lower his eyes from before that steady, self-assured, cool gaze. He longed to look at her ; but when it came to the point, he simply could not keep his eyes steadily fixed on those unwavering eyes of hers.

'Perhaps you're used to dogs,' she went on. 'Have you got one of your own ?'

'N-no,' Peter managed to say.

'Ah, well, that makes it all the braver,' said Husky. Then, noticing that Coo had found the money she had been looking for, she took the boy's hand and shook it, heartily. 'Well, good-bye,' she said, smiling more exquisitely than ever. 'We're so awfully grateful to you. Most awfully,' she repeated. And as she did so, she wondered why she used that word 'awfully' so often. Ordinarily she hardly ever used it. It had seemed suitable somehow, when she was talking with this creature. She was always very hearty and emphatic and schoolboyishly slangy when she was with the lower classes.

'G-g-g . . .' began Peter. Could they be going, he wondered in an agony, suddenly waking out of his comfortable and rosy dream. Really going, without asking him to tea or giving him their addresses? He wanted to implore them to stop a little longer, to let him see them again. But he knew that he wouldn't be able to utter the necessary words. In the face of Husky's good-bye he felt like a man who sees some fearful catastrophe impending and can do nothing to arrest it. 'G-g . . .' he feebly stuttered. But he found himself shaking hands with the other one before he had got to the end of that fatal good-bye.

'You were really splendid,' said Coo, as she shook his hand. 'Really splendid. And you simply must go to a chemist and have the bite disinfected at once. Good-bye, and thank you very, very much.' As she spoke these last words she slipped a neatly folded one-pound note into his palm and with her two hands shut his fingers over it. 'Thank you *so* much,' she repeated.

Violently blushing, Peter shook his head. 'N-n . . .,' he began, and tried to make her take the note back.

But she only smiled more sweetly. 'Yes, yes,' she insisted. 'Please.' And without waiting to hear any more, she turned and ran lightly after Husky, who had walked on, up the path, leading the reluctant Pongo, who still barked and strained heraldically at his leash.

'Well, that's all right,' she said, as she came up with her companion.

' He accepted it ? ' asked Husky.

' Yes, yes.' She nodded. Then changing her tone, ' Let me see,' she went on, ' what were we saying when this wretched dog interrupted us ? '

' N-no,' Peter managed to say at last. But she had already turned and was hurrying away. He took a couple of strides in pursuit ; then checked himself. It was no good. It would only lead to further humiliation if he tried to explain. Why, they might even think, while he was standing there, straining to bring out his words, that he had run after them to ask for more. They might slip another pound into his hand and hurry away still faster. He watched them till they were out of sight, over the brow of the hill ; then turned back towards the Serpentine.

In his imagination he re-acted the scene, not as it had really happened, but as it ought to have happened. When Coo slipped the note into his hand he smiled and courteously returned it, saying : ' I 'm afraid you 've made a mistake. A quite justifiable mistake, I admit. For I look poor, and indeed I am poor. But I am a gentleman, you know. My father was a doctor in Rochdale. My mother was a doctor's daughter. I went to a good school till my people died. They died when I was sixteen, within a few months of one another. So I had to go to work before

I 'd finished my schooling. But you see that I can't take your money.' And then, becoming more gallant, personal and confidential, he went on : ' I separated those beastly dogs because I wanted to do something for you and your friend. Because I thought you so beautiful and wonderful. So that even if I weren't a gentleman, I wouldn't take your money.' Coo was deeply touched by this little speech. She shook him by the hand and told him how sorry she was. And he put her at her ease by assuring her that her mistake had been perfectly comprehensible. And then she asked if he 'd care to come along with them and take a cup of tea. And from this point onwards Peter's imaginings became vaguer and rosier, till he was dreaming the old familiar dream of the peer's daughter, the grateful widow and the lonely orphan ; only there happened to be two goddesses this time, and their faces, instead of being dim creations of fancy, were real and definite.

But he knew, even in the midst of his dreaming, that things hadn't happened like this. He knew that she had gone before he could say anything ; and that even if he had run after them and tried to make his speech of explanation, he could never have done it. For example, he would have had to say that his father was a ' medico,' not a doctor (m being an easier letter than d). And when it came

to telling them that his people had died, he
would have had to say that they had ' perished '
—which would sound facetious, as though
he were trying to make a joke of it. No, no,
the truth must be faced. He had taken the
money and they had gone away thinking that
he was just some sort of a street loafer, who
had risked a bite for the sake of a good tip.
They hadn't even dreamed of treating him
as an equal. As for asking him to tea and
making him their friend . . .

But his fancy was still busy. It struck
him that it had been quite unnecessary to
make any explanation. He might simply
have forced the note back into her hand,
without saying a word. Why hadn't he done
it ? He had to excuse himself for his remiss-
ness. She had slipped away too quickly ;
that was the reason.

Or what if he had walked on ahead of them
and ostentatiously given the money to the
first street-boy he happened to meet ? A
good idea, that. Unfortunately it had not
occurred to him at the time.

All that afternoon Peter walked and walked,
thinking of what had happened, imagining
creditable and satisfying alternatives. But
all the time he knew that these alternatives
were only fanciful. Sometimes the recollection of his humiliation was so vivid that it
made him physically wince and shudder.

The light began to fail. In the grey and violet twilight the lovers pressed closer together as they walked, more frankly clasped one another beneath the trees. Strings of yellow lamps blossomed in the increasing darkness. High up in the pale sky overhead, a quarter of the moon made itself visible. He felt unhappier and lonelier than ever.

His bitten hand was by this time extremely painful. He left the Park and walked along Oxford Street till he found a chemist. When his hand had been disinfected and bandaged he went into a tea-shop and ordered a poached e, g, g, a roll, and a mug of mocha, which he had to translate for the benefit of the uncomprehending waitress as a c, u, p of c, o, f, f, e, e.

'You seem to think I 'm a loafer or a tout.' That 's what he ought to have said to her, indignantly and proudly. 'You 've insulted me. If you were a man, I 'd knock you down. Take your dirty money.' But then, he reflected, he could hardly have expected them to become his friends, after that. On second thoughts, he decided that indignation would have been no good.

'Hurt your hand?' asked the waitress sympathetically, as she set down his egg and his mug of mocha.

Peter nodded. 'B-bitten by a d-d . . . by a h-h-hound.' The word burst out at last, explosively.

Remembered shame made him blush as he spoke. Yes, they had taken him for a tout, they had treated him as though he didn't really exist, as though he were just an instrument whose services you hired and to which, when the bill had been paid, you gave no further thought. The remembrance of humiliation was so vivid, the realization of it so profound and complete, that it affected not only his mind but his body too. His heart beat with unusual rapidity and violence ; he felt sick. It was with the greatest difficulty that he managed to eat his egg and drink his mug of mocha.

Still remembering the painful reality, still feverishly constructing his fanciful alternatives to it, Peter left the tea-shop and, though he was very tired, resumed his aimless walking. He walked along Oxford Street as far as the Circus, turned down Regent Street, halted in Piccadilly to look at the epileptically twitching sky-signs, walked up Shaftesbury Avenue, and turning southwards made his way through by-streets towards the Strand.

In a street near Covent Garden a woman brushed against him. ' Cheer up, dearie,' she said. ' Don't look so glum.'

Peter looked at her in astonishment. Was it possible that she should have been speaking to him ? A woman—was it possible ? He knew, of course, that she was what people called a bad woman. But the fact that she should have spoken to him seemed none the less extraordinary ; and he did not connect it, somehow, with her ' badness.'

' Come along with me,' she wheedled.

Peter nodded. He could not believe it was true. She took his arm.

' You got money ? ' she asked anxiously.

He nodded again.

' You look as though you 'd been to a funeral,' said the woman.

' I 'm l-lonely,' he explained. He felt ready to weep. He even longed to weep— to weep and to be comforted. His voice trembled as he spoke.

' Lonely ? That 's funny. A nice-looking boy like you 's got no call to be lonely.' She laughed significantly and without mirth.

Her bedroom was dimly and pinkly lighted. A smell of cheap scent and unwashed under-linen haunted the air.

' Wait a tick,' she said, and disappeared through a door into an inner room.

He sat there, waiting. A minute later she returned, wearing a kimono and bedroom slippers. She sat on his knees, threw her arms round his neck and began to kiss him. ' Lovey,' she said in her cracked voice, ' lovey.' Her eyes were hard and cold. Her breath smelt of spirits. Seen at close range she was indescribably horrible.

Peter saw her, it seemed to him, for the first time—saw and completely realized her. He averted his face. Remembering the peer's daughter who had sprained her ankle, the lonely orphan, the widow whose child had tumbled into the Round Pond ; remembering Coo and Husky, he untwined her arms, he pushed her away from him, he sprang to his feet.

'S-sorry,' he said. 'I must g-g . . . I'd forg-gotten something. I . . .' He picked up his hat and moved towards the door.

The woman ran after him and caught him by the arm. 'You young devil, you,' she screamed. Her abuse was horrible and filthy. 'Asking a girl and then trying to sneak away without paying. Oh, no you don't, no you don't. You . . .'

And the abuse began again.

Peter dipped his hand into his pocket, and pulled out Coo's neatly folded note. 'L-let me g-go,' he said as he gave it her.

While she was suspiciously unfolding it, he hurried away, slamming the door behind him, and ran down the dark stairs, into the street.

# THE MONOCLE

THE drawing-room was on the first floor. The indistinct, inarticulate noise of many voices floated down the stairs, like the roaring of a distant train. Gregory took off his greatcoat and handed it to the parlour-maid.

'Don't trouble to show me up,' he said. 'I know the way.'

Always so considerate ! And yet, for some reason, servants would never do anything for him ; they despised and disliked him.

'Don't bother,' he insisted.

The parlour-maid, who was young, with high colours and yellow hair, looked at him, he thought, with silent contempt and walked away. In all probability, he reflected, she had never meant to show him up. He felt humiliated—yet once more.

A mirror hung at the bottom of the stairs. He peered at his image, gave his hair a pat, his tie a straightening touch. His face was smooth and egg-shaped ; he had regular features, pale hair and a very small mouth, with cupid's bow effects in the upper lip. A curate's face. Secretly, he thought himself handsome and was always astonished that more people were not of his opinion.

Gregory mounted the stairs, polishing his monocle as he went. The volume of sound increased. At the landing, where the staircase turned, he could see the open door of the drawing-room. At first he could see only the upper quarter of the tall doorway and, through it, a patch of ceiling ; but with every step he saw more—a strip of wall below the cornice, a picture, the heads of people, their whole bodies, their legs and feet. At the penultimate step, he inserted his monocle and replaced his handkerchief in his pocket. Squaring his shoulders, he marched in—almost militarily, he flattered himself. His hostess was standing near the window, at the other side of the room. He advanced towards her, already, though she had not yet seen him, mechanically smiling his greetings. The room was crowded, hot, and misty with cigarette smoke. The noise was almost palpable ; Gregory felt as though he were pushing his way laboriously through some denser element. Neck-deep, he waded through noise, still holding preciously above the flood his smile. He presented it, intact, to his hostess.

' Good evening, Hermione.'

' Ah, Gregory. How delightful ! Good evening.'

' I adore your dress,' said Gregory, conscientiously following the advice of the enviably successful friend who had told him that one should never neglect to pay a compliment, however manifestly insincere. It wasn't a bad dress, for that matter. But, of course, poor dear Hermione contrived to ruin anything she put on. She was quite malignantly ungraceful and ugly—on purpose, it always seemed to Gregory. ' Too lovely,' he cooed in his rather high voice.

Hermione smiled with pleasure. ' I 'm so glad,' she began. But before she could get any further, a loud voice, nasally chanting, interrupted her.

' Behold the monster Polypheme, behold the monster Polypheme,' it quoted, musically, from *Acis and Galatea*.

Gregory flushed. A large hand slapped him in the middle of the back, below the shoulder blades. His body emitted the drum-like thud of a patted retriever.

' Well, Polypheme ' ; the voice had ceased to sing and was conversational—' well, Polypheme, how are you ? '

' Very well, thanks,' Gregory replied, without looking round. It was that drunken South African brute, Paxton. ' Very well, thanks, Silenus,' he added.

Paxton had called him Polypheme because of his monocle : Polypheme, the one-eyed, wheel-eyed Cyclops. Tit for mythological tat. In future, he would always call Paxton Silenus.

' Bravo ! ' shouted Paxton. Gregory winced and gasped under a second, heartier slap. ' Pretty high-class, this party. Eh,

Hermione ?   Pretty cultured, what ?   It isn't every day that a hostess can hear her guests shooting Greco-Roman witticisms at one another.   I congratulate you, Hermione.'   He put his arm round her waist.   ' I congratulate you on us.'

Hermione disengaged herself.   ' Don't be a bore, Paxton,' she said impatiently.

Paxton laughed theatrically.   ' Ha, ha ! ' A villain's laugh on the melodrama stage. And it was not his laughter only that was theatrical ;   his whole person parodied the old-time tragedian.   The steep aquiline profile, the deeply sunken eyes, the black hair worn rather long—they were characteristic. ' A thousand apologies ' :  he spoke with an ironical courtesy.   ' The poor colonial forgets himself.   Boozy and ill-mannered boor ! '

' Idiot ! ' said Hermione, and moved away.

Gregory made a movement to follow her, but Paxton caught him by the sleeve.   ' Tell me,' he enquired earnestly, ' why *do* you wear a monocle, Polypheme ? '

' Well, if you really want to know,' Gregory answered stiffly, ' for the simple reason that I happen to be short-sighted and astigmatic in the left eye and not in the right.'

' Short-sighted and astigmatic ? ' the other repeated in tones of affected astonishment. ' Short-sighted and astigmatic ?   God forgive me—and I thought it was because you wanted to look like a duke on the musical-comedy stage.'

Gregory's laugh was meant to be one of frankly amazed amusement. That any one should have imagined such a thing ! Incredible, comical ! But a note of embarrassment and discomfort sounded through the amusement. For in reality, of course, Paxton was so devilishly nearly right. Conscious, only too acutely, of his nullity, his provincialism, his lack of successful arrogance, he had made the oculist's diagnosis an excuse for trying to look smarter, more insolent, and impressive. In vain. His eyeglass had done nothing to increase his self-confidence. He was never at ease when he wore it. Monocle-wearers, he decided, are like poets : born, not made. Cambridge had not eradicated the midland grammar-school boy. Cultured, with literary leanings, he was always aware of being the wealthy boot manufacturer's heir. He could not get used to his monocle. Most of the time, in spite of the oculist's recommendations, it dangled at the end of its string, a pendulum when he walked and involving itself messily, when he ate, in soup and tea, in marmalade and the butter. It was only occasionally, in specially favourable circumstances, that Gregory adjusted it to his eye ; more rarely still that he kept it, once adjusted, more than a few minutes, a few seconds even, without raising his eyebrow and letting it fall again. And how seldom circumstances *were* favourable to Gregory's eyeglass ! Sometimes his environment was too sordid for it, sometimes too smart. To wear a monocle in the presence of the poor, the miserable, the analphabetic is too triumphantly pointed a comment on their lot. Moreover, the poor and the analphabetic have a most deplorable habit of laughing derisively at such symbols of superior caste. Gregory was not laughter-proof ; he lacked the lordly confidence and unawareness of nature's monocle-wearers. He did not know how to ignore the poor, to treat them, if it were absolutely necessary to have dealings with them, as machines or domestic animals. He had seen too much of them in the days when his father was alive and had compelled him to take a practical interest in the business. It was the same lack of confidence that made him almost as chary of fixing his eyeglass in the presence of the rich. With them, he never felt quite sure that he had a right to his monocle. He felt himself a parvenu to monocularity. And then there were the intelligent. Their company, too, was most unfavourable to the eyeglass. Eyeglassed, how could one talk of serious things ? ' Mozart,' you might say, for example, ' Mozart is so pure, so spiritually beautiful.' It was unthinkable to speak those words with a disk of crystal screwed into your left eye-socket. No, the environment was only too rarely favourable. Still, benignant circumstances did sometimes present themselves. Hermione's half-Bohemian parties, for example. But he had reckoned without Paxton.

Amused, amazed, he laughed. As though by accident, the monocle dropped from his eye. ' Oh, put it back,' cried Paxton, ' put it back, I implore you,' and himself caught the glass, where it dangled over Gregory's stomach, and tried to replace it.

Gregory stepped back ; with one hand he pushed away his persecutor, with the other he tried to snatch the monocle from between his fingers. Paxton would not let it go.

' I implore you,' Paxton kept repeating.

' Give it me at once,' said Gregory, furiously, but in a low voice, so that people should not look round and see the grotesque cause of the quarrel. He had never been so outrageously made a fool of.

Paxton gave it him at last. ' Forgive me,' he said, with mock penitence. ' Forgive a poor drunken colonial who doesn't know what 's done in the best society and what isn't. You must remember I 'm only a boozer, just a poor, hard-working drunkard. You know those registration forms they give you in French hotels ? Name, date of birth and so on. You know ? '

Gregory nodded, with dignity.

'Well, when it comes to profession, I always write "ivrogne." That is, when I'm sober enough to remember the French word. If I'm too far gone, I just put "Drunkard." They all know English, nowadays.'

'Oh,' said Gregory coldly.

'It's a capital profession,' Paxton confided. 'It permits you to do whatever you like— any damned thing that comes into your head. Throw your arms round any woman you fancy, tell her the most gross and fantastic impertinences, insult the men, laugh in people's faces —everything's permitted to the poor drunkard, particularly if he's only a poor colonial and doesn't know any better. *Verb. sap.* Take the hint from me, old boy. Drop the monocle. It's no damned good. Be a boozer ; you'll have much more fun. Which reminds me that I must go and find some more drink at all costs. I'm getting sober.'

He disappeared into the crowd. Relieved, Gregory looked round in search of familiar faces. As he looked, he polished his monocle, took the opportunity to wipe his forehead, then put the glass to his eye.

'Excuse me.' He oozed his way insinuatingly between the close-set chairs, passed like a slug ('Excuse me') between the all but contiguous backs of two standing groups. 'Excuse me.' He had seen acquaintances

228

over there, by the fireplace : Ransom and
Mary Haig and Miss Camperdown. He
joined in their conversation : they were talking
about Mrs. Mandragore.

All the old familiar stories about that
famous lion-huntress were being repeated.
He himself repeated two or three, with suitable
pantomime, perfected by a hundred tellings.
In the middle of a grimace, at the top of an
elaborate gesture, he suddenly saw himself
grimacing, gesticulating, he suddenly heard
the cadences of his voice repeating, by heart,
the old phrases. Why does one come to
parties, why on earth ? Always the same
boring people, the same dull scandal, and one's
own same parlour tricks. Each time. But
he smirked, he mimed, he fluted and bellowed
his story through to the end. His auditors
even laughed ; it was a success. But Gregory
felt ashamed of himself. Ransom began
telling the story of Mrs. Mandragore and the
Maharajah of Pataliapur. He groaned in the
spirit. Why ? he asked himself, why, why,
why ? Behind him, they were talking politics.
Still pretending to smile at the Mandragore
fable, he listened.

' It's the beginning of the end,' the politician was saying, prophesying destructions
in a loud and cheerful voice.

' " Dear Maharajah," ' Ransom imitated
the Mandragore's intense voice, her aimed

and yearning gestures, ' " if you knew how I *adore* the East." '

' Our unique position was due to the fact that we started the industrial system before any one else. Now, when the rest of the world has followed our example, we find it 's a disadvantage to have started first. All our equipment is old-fash——'

' Gregory,' called Mary Haig, ' what 's your story about the Unknown Soldier ? '

' Unknown Soldier ? ' said Gregory vaguely, trying to catch what was being said behind him.

' The latest arrivals have the latest machinery. It 's obvious. We . . .'

' You know the one. The Mandragore's party ; you know.'

' Oh, when she asked us all to tea to meet the Mother of the Unknown Soldier.'

' . . . like Italy,' the politician was saying in his loud, jolly voice. ' In future, we shall always have one or two millions more population than we can employ. Living on the State.'

One or two millions. He thought of the Derby. Perhaps there might be a hundred thousand in that crowd. Ten Derbies, twenty Derbies, all half-starved, walking through the streets with brass bands and banners. He let his monocle fall. Must send five pounds to the London Hospital, he thought. Four thousand eight hundred a year. Thirteen pounds a day. Less taxes, of course. Taxes were terrible. Monstrous, sir, monstrous. He tried to feel as indignant about taxes as those old gentlemen who get red in the face when they talk about them. But somehow, he couldn't manage to do it. And after all, taxes were no excuse, no justification. He felt all at once profoundly depressed. Still, he tried to comfort himself, not more than twenty or twenty-five out of the two million could live on his income. Twenty-five out of two millions—it was absurd, derisory! But he was not consoled.

'And the odd thing is,' Ransom was still talking about the Mandragore, 'she isn't really in the least interested in her lions. She'll begin telling you about what Anatole France said to her and then forget in the middle, out of pure boredom, what she's talking about.'

Oh, God, God, thought Gregory. How often had he heard Ransom making the same reflections on the Mandragore's psychology! How often! He'd be bringing out that bit about the chimpanzees in half a moment. God help us!

'Have you ever watched the chimpanzees at the Zoo?' said Ransom. 'The way they pick up a straw or a banana skin and examine it for a few seconds with a passionate attention.' He went through a simian pantomime. 'Then, suddenly, get utterly bored, let the thing drop

from their fingers and look round vaguely in
search of something else. They always re-
mind me of the Mandragore and her guests.
The way she begins, earnestly, as though you
were the only person in the world ; then all
at once . . .'

Gregory could bear it no longer. He
mumbled something to Miss Camperdown
about having seen somebody he must talk to,
and disappeared, ' Excuse me,' slug-like,
through the crowd. Oh, the misery, the
appalling gloom of it all ! In a corner, he
found young Crane and two or three other
men with tumblers in their hands.

' Ah, Crane,' he said, ' for God's sake tell
me where you got that drink.'

That golden fluid—it seemed the only hope.
Crane pointed in the direction of the archway
leading into the back drawing-room. He
raised his glass without speaking, drank, and
winked at Gregory over the top of it. He had
a face that looked like an accident. Gregory
oozed on through the crowd. ' Excuse me,'
he said aloud ; but inwardly he was saying,
' God help us.'

At the further end of the back drawing-
room was a table with bottles and glasses.
The professional drunkard was sitting on a
sofa near by, glass in hand, making personal
remarks to himself about all the people who
came within earshot.

'Christ !' he was saying, as Gregory came up to the table. 'Christ ! Look at that !' *That* was the gaunt Mrs. Labadie in cloth of gold and pearls. 'Christ !' She had pounced on a shy young man entrenched behind the table.

'Tell me, Mr. Foley,' she began, approaching her horse-like face very close to that of the young man and speaking appealingly, 'you who know *all* about mathematics, tell me . . .'

'Is it possible ?' exclaimed the professional drunkard. 'In England's green and pleasant land ? Ha, ha, ha !' He laughed his melodramatic laugh.

Pretentious fool, thought Gregory. How romantic he thinks himself ! The laughing philosopher, what ? Drunk because the world isn't good enough for him. Quite the little Faust.

'And Polypheme too,' Paxton soliloquized on, 'funny little Polypheme !' He laughed again. 'The heir to all the ages. Christ !'

With dignity, Gregory poured himself out some whisky and filled up the glass from the siphon—with dignity, with conscious grace and precision, as though he were acting the part of a man who helps himself to whisky and soda on the stage. He took a sip ; then elaborately acted the part of one who takes out his handkerchief and blows his nose.

'Don't they make one believe in birth

control, all these people,' continued the professional drunkard. ' If only their parents could have had a few intimate words with Stopes ! Heigh ho ! ' He uttered a stylized Shakespearean sigh.

Buffoon, thought Gregory. And the worst is that if one called him one, he 'd pretend that he 'd said so himself, all the time. And so he has, of course, just to be on the safe side. But in reality, it 's obvious, the man thinks of himself as a sort of Musset or up-to-date Byron. A beautiful soul, darkened and embittered by experience. Ugh !

Still pretending to be unaware of the professional boozer's proximity, Gregory went through the actions of the man who sips.

' How *clear* you make it ! ' Mrs. Labadie was saying, point blank, into the young mathematician's face. She smiled at him ; the horse, thought Gregory, has a terribly human expression.

' Well,' said the young mathematician nervously, ' now we come on to Riemann.'

' Riemann ! ' Mrs. Labadie repeated, with a kind of ecstasy. ' Riemann ! ' as though the geometrician's soul were in his name.

Gregory wished that there were somebody to talk to, somebody who would relieve him of the necessity of acting the part of unaware indifference before the scrutinizing eyes of Paxton. He leaned against the wall in the attitude of one who falls, all of a sudden, into a brown study. Blankly and pensively, he stared at a point on the opposite wall, high up, just below the ceiling. People must be wondering, he reflected, what he was thinking about. And what was he thinking about? Himself. Vanity, vanity. Oh, the gloom, the misery of it all !

' Polypheme ! '

He pretended not to hear.

' Polypheme ! '   It was a shout this time.

Gregory slightly overacted the part of one who is suddenly aroused from profoundest meditation. He started ; blinking, a little dazed, he turned his head.

' Ah, Paxton,' he said.  ' Silenus ! I hadn't noticed that you were there.'

' Hadn't  you ? '  said  the  professional drunkard.  ' That was damned clever of you. What were you thinking about so picturesquely there ? '

' Oh, nothing,' said Gregory, smiling with the modest confusion of the Thinker, caught in the act.

' Just  what  I  imagined,'  said  Paxton. ' Nothing. Nothing at all. Jesus Christ ! ' he added, for himself.

Gregory's smile was rather sickly. He averted his face and passed once more into meditation. It seemed, in the circumstances, the best thing he could do. Dreamily, as though unconscious of what he was doing, he emptied his glass.

' Crippen ! ' he heard the professional drunkard muttering. ' It 's like a funeral. Joyless, joyless.'

' Well, Gregory.'

Gregory did another of his graceful starts, his dazed blinkings. He had been afraid, for a moment, that Spiller was going to respect his meditation and not speak to him. That would have been very embarrassing.

' Spiller ! ' he exclaimed with delight and astonishment. ' My dear chap.' He shook him heartily by the hand.

Square-faced, with a wide mouth and an immense forehead, framed in copious and curly hair, Spiller looked like a Victorian celebrity. His friends declared that he might actually have been a Georgian celebrity but for the fact that he preferred talking to writing.

' Just up for the day,' explained Spiller. ' I couldn't stand another hour of the bloody country. Working all day. No company but my own. I find I bore myself to death.' He helped himself to whisky.

' Jesus ! The great man ! Ha, ha ! ' The professional drunkard covered his face with his hands and shuddered violently.

' Do you mean to say you came specially for this ? ' asked Gregory, waving his hand to indicate the party at large.

'Not specially. Incidentally. I heard that Hermione was giving a party, so I dropped in.'

'Why *does* one go to parties ?' said Gregory, unconsciously assuming something of the embittered Byronic manner of the professional drunkard.

'To satisfy the cravings of the herd instinct.' Spiller replied to the rhetorical question without hesitation and with a pontifical air of infallibility. 'Just as one pursues women to satisfy the cravings of the reproductive instinct.' Spiller had an impressive way of making everything he said sound very scientific ; it all seemed to come straight from the horse's mouth, so to speak. Vague-minded Gregory found him most stimulating.

'You mean, one goes to parties just in order to be in a crowd ?'

'Precisely,' Spiller replied. 'Just to feel the warmth of the herd around one and sniff the smell of one's fellow-humans.' He snuffed the thick, hot air.

'I suppose you must be right,' said Gregory. 'It 's certainly very hard to think of any other reason.'

He looked round the room as though searching for other reasons. And surprisingly, he found one : Molly Voles. He had not seen her before ; she must have only just arrived.

237

'I 've got a capital idea for a new paper,' began Spiller.

'Have you?' Gregory did not show much curiosity. How beautiful her neck was, and those thin arms!

'Art, literature, and science,' Spiller continued. 'The idea 's a really modern one. It 's to bring science into touch with the arts and so into touch with life. Life, art, science —all three would gain. You see the notion?'

'Yes,' said Gregory, 'I see.' He was looking at Molly, hoping to catch her eye. He caught it at last, that cool and steady grey eye. She smiled and nodded.

'You like the idea?' asked Spiller.

'I think it 's splendid,' answered Gregory with a sudden warmth that astonished his interlocutor.

Spiller's large severe face shone with pleasure. 'Oh, I 'm glad,' he said, 'I 'm very glad indeed that you like it so much.'

'I think it 's splendid,' said Gregory extravagantly. 'Simply splendid.' She had seemed really glad to see him, he thought.

'I was thinking,' Spiller pursued, with a rather elaborate casualness of manner, 'I was thinking you might like to help me start the thing. One could float it comfortably with a thousand pounds of capital.'

The enthusiasm faded out of Gregory's face: it became blank in its clerical roundness. He

shook his head. ' If I had a thousand pounds,'
he said regretfully. Damn the man ! he was
thinking. Setting me a trap like that.

' If,' repeated Spiller. ' But, my dear
fellow ! ' He laughed. ' And besides, it 's
a safe six per cent. investment. I can collect
an extraordinarily strong set of contributors,
you know.'

Gregory shook his head once more. ' Alas,'
he said, ' alas ! '

' And what 's more,' insisted Spiller, ' you 'd
be a benefactor of society.'

' Impossible.' Gregory was firm ; he
planted his feet like a donkey and would not
be moved. Money was the one thing he
never had a difficulty in being firm about.

' But come,' said Spiller, ' come. What 's
a thousand pounds to a millionaire like you ?
You 've got—how much *have* you got ? '

Gregory stared him glassily in the eyes.

' Twelve hundred a year,' he said. ' Say
fourteen hundred.' He could see that Spiller
didn't believe him. Damn the man ! Not
that he really expected him to believe ; but
still . . . ' And then there are one's taxes,'
he added plaintively, ' and one's contributions
to charities.' He remembered that fiver he
was going to send to the London Hospital.
' The London Hospital, for example—always
short of money.' He shook his head sadly.
' Quite impossible, I 'm afraid.' He thought

of all the unemployed ; ten Derby crowds, half starved, with banners and brass bands. He felt himself blushing. Damn the man ! He was furious with Spiller.

Two voices sounded simultaneously in his ears : the professional drunkard's and another, a woman's—Molly's.

' The succubus ! ' groaned the professional drunkard. ' Il ne manquait que ça ! '

' Impossible ? ' said Molly's voice, un-expectedly repeating his latest word. ' What 's impossible ? '

' Well——' said Gregory, embarrassed, and hesitated.

It was Spiller who explained.

' Why, of course Gregory can put up a thousand pounds,' said Molly, when she had learned what was the subject at issue. She looked at him indignantly, contemptuously, as though reproaching him for his avarice.

' You know better than I, then,' said Gregory, trying to take the airy jocular line about the matter. He remembered what the enviably successful friend had told him about compliments. ' How lovely you look in that white dress, Molly ! ' he added, and tempered the jocularity of his smile with a glance that was meant to be at once insolent and tender. ' Too lovely,' he repeated, and put up his monocle to look at her.

' Thank you,' she said, looking back at him

unwaveringly. Her eyes were calm and bright. Against that firm and penetrating regard his jocularity, his attempt at insolent tenderness, punctured and crumpled up. He averted his eyes, he let fall his eyeglass. It was a weapon he did not dare or know how to use—it made him look ridiculous. He was like horse-faced Mrs. Labadie flirting coquettishly with her fan.

'I'd like to discuss the question in any case,' he said to Spiller, glad of any excuse to escape from those eyes. 'But I assure you I really can't. . . . Not the whole thousand, at any rate,' he added, feeling despairingly that he had been forced against his will to surrender.

'Molly!' shouted the professional drunkard.

Obediently she went and sat down beside him on the sofa.

'Well, Tom,' she said, and laid her hand on his knee. 'How are you?'

'As I always am, when you're anywhere about,' answered the professional drunkard tragically: 'insane.' He put his arm round her shoulders and leaned towards her. 'Utterly insane.'

'I'd rather we didn't sit like this, you know.' She smiled at him; they looked at one another closely. Then Paxton withdrew his arm and leaned back in his corner of the sofa.

Looking at them, Gregory was suddenly

convinced that they were lovers. We needs
must love the lowest when we see it. All
Molly's lovers were like that : ruffians.

He turned to Spiller. ' Shouldn't we go
back to my rooms ? ' he suggested, interrupting him in the midst of a long explanatory
discourse about the projected paper. ' It 'll
be quieter there and less stuffy.' Molly and
Paxton, Molly and that drunken brute. Was
it possible ? It was certain : he had no
doubts. ' Let 's get out of this beastly place
quickly,' he added.

' All right,' Spiller agreed. ' One last
lashing of whisky to support us on the way.'
He reached for the bottle.

Gregory drank nearly half a tumbler, un-
diluted. A few yards down the street, he
realized that he was rather tipsy.

' I think I must have a very feebly developed
herd instinct,' he said. ' How I hate these
crowds ! ' Molly and Silenus-Paxton ! He
imagined their loves. And he had thought
that she had been glad to see him, when first
he caught her eye.

They emerged into Bedford Square. The
gardens were as darkly mysterious as a piece
of country woodland. Woodland without,
whisky within, combined to make Gregory's
melancholy vocal. *Che farò senz' Euridice ?*
he softly sang.

' You can do without her very well,' said

Spiller, replying to the quotation. 'That's the swindle and stupidity of love. Each time you feel convinced that it's something immensely significant and everlasting : you feel infinitely. Each time. Three weeks later you're beginning to find her boring ; or somebody else rolls the eye and the infinite emotions are transferred and you're off on another eternal week-end. It's a sort of practical joke. Very stupid and disagreeable. But then nature's humour isn't ours.'

'You think it's a joke, that infinite feeling ?' asked Gregory indignantly. 'I don't. I believe that it represents something real, outside ourselves, something in the structure of the universe.'

'A different universe with every mistress, eh ?'

'But if it occurs only once in a lifetime ?' asked Gregory in a maudlin voice. He longed to tell his companion how unhappy he felt about Molly, how much unhappier than anybody had ever felt before.

'It doesn't,' said Spiller.

'But if I say it does ?' Gregory hiccoughed.

'That's only due to lack of opportunities,' Spiller replied in his most decisively scientific, *ex cathedra* manner.

'I don't agree with you,' was all that Gregory could say, feebly. He decided not to mention his unhappiness. Spiller might not be a sympathetic listener. . Coarse old devil !

' Personally,' Spiller continued, ' I 've long ago ceased trying to make sense of it. I just accept these infinite emotions for what they are—very stimulating and exciting while they last—and don't attempt to rationalize or explain them. It 's the only sane and scientific way of treating the facts.'

There was a silence. They had emerged into the brilliance of the Tottenham Court Road. The polished roadway reflected the arc lamps. The entrances to the cinema palaces were caverns of glaring yellow light. A pair of buses roared past.

' They 're dangerous, those infinite emotions,' Spiller went on, ' very dangerous. I once came within an inch of getting married on the strength of one of them. It began on a steamer. You know what steamers are. The extraordinary aphrodisiac effects sea voyaging has on people who aren't used to it, especially women ! They really ought to be studied by some competent physiologist. Of course, it may be simply the result of idleness, high feeding and constant proximity— though I doubt if you 'd get the same results in similar circumstances on land. Perhaps the total change of environment, from earth to water, undermines the usual terrestrial prejudices. Perhaps the very shortness of the voyage helps—the sense that it's so soon coming to an end that rosebuds must be gathered and hay made while the sun shines. Who knows?' He shrugged his shoulders. ' But in any case, it's most extraordinary. Well, it began, as I say, on a steamer.'

Gregory listened. A few minutes since the trees of Bedford Square had waved in the darkness of his boozily maudlin soul. The lights, the noise, the movement of the Tottenham Court Road were now behind his eyes as well as before them. He listened, grinning. The story lasted well into the Charing Cross Road.

By the time it had come to an end, Gregory was feeling in an entirely jolly and jaunty mood. He had associated himself with Spiller; Spiller's adventures were his. He guffawed with laughter, he readjusted his monocle, which had been dangling all this time at the end of its string, which had been tinkling at every step against the buttons of his waistcoat. (A broken heart, it must be obvious to any one who has the slightest sensibility, cannot possibly wear an eyeglass.) He too was a bit of a dog, now. He hiccoughed; a certain suspicion of queasiness tempered his jollity, but it was no more than the faintest suspicion. Yes, yes; he too knew all about life on steamers, even though the longest of his sea voyages had only been from Newhaven to Dieppe.

When they reached Cambridge Circus, the theatres were just disgorging their audiences. The pavements were crowded ; the air was full of noise and the perfume of women. Overhead, the sky-signs winced and twitched. The theatre vestibules brightly glared. It was an unaristocratic and vulgar luxury, to which Gregory had no difficulty in feeling himself superior. Through his Cyclopean monocle, he gazed enquiringly at every woman they passed. He felt wonderfully reckless (the queasiness was the merest suspicion of an unpleasant sensation), wonderfully jolly and— yes, that was curious—large : larger than life. As for Molly Voles, he 'd teach her.

' Lovely creature, that,' he said, indicating a cloak of pink silk and gold, a close-cropped golden head.

Spiller nodded, indifferently. ' About that paper of ours,' he said thoughtfully. ' I was thinking that we might start off with a series of articles on the metaphysical basis of science, the reasons, historical and philosophical, that we have for assuming that scientific truth is true.'

' H'm,' said Gregory.

' And concurrently a series on the meaning and point of art. Start right from the beginning in both cases. Quite a good idea, don't you think ? '

' Quite,' said Gregory. One of his monocular glances had been received with a smile of invitation ; she was ugly, unfortunately, and obviously professional. Haughtily he glared past her, as though she were not there.

' But whether Tolstoy was right,' Spiller was meditatively saying, ' I never feel sure. Is it true, what he says, that the function of art is the conveyance of emotion ? In part, I should say, but not exclusively, not exclusively.' He shook his large head.

' I seem to be getting tipsier,' said Gregory, more to himself than to his companion. He still walked correctly, but he was conscious, too conscious, of the fact. And the suspicion of queasiness was becoming well founded.

Spiller did not hear or, hearing, ignored the remark. ' For me,' he continued, ' the main function of art is to impart knowledge. The artist knows more than the rest of us. He is born knowing more about his soul than we know of ours, and more about the relations existing between his soul and the cosmos. He anticipates what will be common knowledge in a higher state of development. Most of our moderns are primitives compared with the most advanced of the dead.'

' Quite,' said Gregory, not listening. His thoughts were elsewhere, with his eyes.

' Moreover,' Spiller went on, ' he can say what he knows, and say it in such a way that our own rudimentary, incoherent, unrealized

knowledge of what he talks about falls into
a kind of pattern—like iron filings under the
influence of the magnet.'

There were three of them—ravishingly,
provocatively young—standing in a group at
the pavement's edge. They chattered, they
stared with bright derisive eyes at the passers-
by, they commented in audible whispers, they
burst into irrepressible shrill laughter. Spiller
and Gregory approached, were spied by one
of the three, who nudged her fellows.

'Oh, Lord !'

They giggled, they laughed aloud, they
were contorted with mockery.

'Look at old Golliwog !' That was for
Spiller, who walked bareheaded, his large
grey hat in his hand.

'And the nut !' Another yell for the
monocle.

'It's that magnetic power,' said Spiller,
quite unaware of the lovely derision of which
he was the object, 'that power of organizing
mental chaos into a pattern, which makes a
truth uttered poetically, in art, more valuable
than a truth uttered scientifically, in prose.'

Playfully reproving, Gregory wagged a
finger at the mockers. There was a yet more
piercing yell. The two men passed ; smil-
ingly Gregory looked back. He felt jauntier
and jollier than ever ; but the suspicion was
ripening to a certainty.

' For instance,' said Spiller, ' I may know well enough that all men are mortal. But this knowledge is organized and given a form, it is even actually increased and deepened, when Shakespeare talks about all our yester-days having lighted fools the way to dusty death.'

Gregory was trying to think of an excuse for giving his companion the slip and turning back to dally with the three. He would love them all, simultaneously.

> La touffe échevelée
> De baisers que les dieux gardaient si bien mêlée.

The Mallarméan phrase came back to him, imposing on his vague desires (old man Spiller was quite right, old imbecile !) the most elegant of forms. Spiller's words came to him as though from a great distance.

' And the *Coriolan* overture is a piece of new knowledge, as well as a composer of existing chaotic knowledge.'

He would suggest dropping in at the Monico, pretext a call of nature, slip out and never return. Old imbecile, maundering on like that ! Not but what it mightn't have been quite interesting, at the right moment. But now . . . And he thought, no doubt, that he was going to tap him, Gregory, for a thousand pounds ! Gregory could have laughed aloud. But his derision was tinged with an uneasy consciousness that his tipsiness had definitely taken a new and disquieting form.

' Some of Cézanne's landscapes,' he heard Spiller saying.

Suddenly, from a shadowed doorway a few yards down the street in front of them, there emerged, slowly, tremulously, a thing : a bundle of black tatters that moved on a pair of old squashed boots, that was topped by a broken, dog's-eared hat. It had a face, clay-coloured and emaciated. It had hands, in one of which it held a little tray with match-boxes. It opened its mouth, from which two or three of the discoloured teeth were missing ; it sang, all but inaudibly. Gregory thought he recognized ' Nearer, my God, to Thee.' They approached.

' Certain frescoes of Giotto, certain early Greek sculptures,' Spiller went on with his interminable catalogue.

The thing looked at them, Gregory looked at the thing. Their eyes met. Gregory expanded his left eye-socket. The monocle dropped to the end of its silken tether. He felt in his right-hand trouser pocket, the pocket where he kept his silver, for a sixpence, a shilling even. The pocket contained only four half-crowns. Half a crown ? He hesitated, drew one of the coins half-way to the surface, then let it fall again with a chink. He dipped his left hand into his other trouser

pocket, he withdrew it, full. Into the proffered tray he dropped three pennies and a
halfpenny.

' No, I don't want any matches,' he said.

Gratitude interrupted the hymn. Gregory
had never felt so much ashamed in his life.
His monocle tinkled against the buttons of
his waistcoat. Deliberately, he placed one
foot before the other, walking with correctness,
but as though on a tight-rope. Yet another
insult to the thing. He wished to God he
were sober. He wished to God he hadn't
desired with such precision that ' dishevelled
tuft of kisses.' Threepence-halfpenny ! But
he could still run back and give half a crown,
two half-crowns. He could still run back.
Step by step, as though on the tight-rope, he
advanced, keeping step with Spiller. Four
steps, five steps . . . eleven steps, twelve
steps, thirteen steps. Oh, the unluckiness !
Eighteen steps, nineteen. . . . Too late ; it
would be ridiculous to turn back now, it would
be too conspicuously silly. Twenty-three,
twenty-four steps. The suspicion was a certainty of queasiness, a growing certainty.

' At the same time,' Spiller was saying, ' I
really don't see how the vast majority of scientific truths and hypotheses can ever become
the subject of art. I don't see how they can
be given poetic, emotive significance without
losing their precision. How could you render

the electro-magnetic theory of light, for example, in a moving literary form ?   It simply can't be done.'

' Oh, for God's sake,' shouted Gregory with a sudden outburst of fury, ' for God's sake, shut up !   How can you go on talking and talking away like this ? '   He hiccoughed again, more profoundly and menacingly than before.

' But why on earth not ? '  asked Spiller with a mild astonishment.

' Talking about art and science and poetry,' said Gregory tragically, almost with tears in his eyes, ' when there are two million people in England on the brink of starvation.   Two million.'   He meant the repetition to be impressive, but he hiccoughed yet once more ; he was feeling definitely rather sick.   ' Living in stinking hovels,' he went on, *decrescendo*, ' promiscuously, herded together, like animals. Worse than animals.'

They had halted ;   they confronted one another.

' How can you ? '  repeated Gregory, trying to reproduce the generous indignation of a moment since.   But anticipations of nausea were creeping up from his stomach, like a miasma from a marsh, filling his mind, driving out from it every thought, every emotion except the horrid apprehension of being sick.

Spiller's large face suddenly lost its monumental, Victorian celebrity's appearance ;   it seemed to fall to pieces. The mouth opened, the eyes puckered up, the forehead broke into wrinkles and the deep lines running from either side of the nose to the corners of the mouth expanded and contracted wildly, like a pair of demented glove-stretchers. An immense sound came out of him. His great body was shaken with gigantic laughter.

Patiently—patience was all that was left him, patience and a fading hope—Gregory waited for the paroxysm to subside. He had made a fool of himself ; he was being derided. But he was past caring.

Spiller so far recovered as to be able to speak. 'You're wonderful, my dear Gregory,' he said, gasping. The tears stood in his eyes. 'Really superb.' He took him affectionately by the arm and, still laughing, walked on. Gregory perforce walked too ; he had no choice.

'If you don't mind,' he said after a few steps, 'I think we'll take a taxi.'

'What, to Jermyn Street ?' said Spiller.

'I think we'd better,' Gregory insisted.

Climbing into the vehicle, he managed to entangle his monocle in the handle of the door. The string snapped : the glass dropped on the floor of the cab. Spiller picked it up and returned it to him.

'Thank you,' said Gregory, and put it out of harm's way into a waistcoat pocket.

# FAIRY GODMOTHER

## I

At 17 Purlieu Villas it was a fairy god-mother's arrival. The enormous Daimler— it looked larger than the house itself—rolled whispering up the street, dark blue and dis-creetly lustrous. (' Like stars on the sea '— the darkly glittering Daimler always reminded Susan of the Hebrew Melodies—' when the blue wave rolls nightly on deep Galilee.') Between lace curtains eyes followed its passage ; it was rarely that forty horses passed these suburban windows. At the gate of Number Seventeen the portent came to a halt. The chauffeur jumped down and opened the door. The fairy godmother emerged.

Mrs. Escobar was tall and slender, so abnormally so, that, fashionably dressed, she looked like a fashion-plate—fabulously elegant, beyond all reality.

She was wearing black to-day—a black suit very thinly piped at the cuffs and collar, at the pockets and along the seams of the skirt, with red. A high muslin stock encased her neck and from it depended an elaborate frill, which projected from between the lapels of her coat like the idly waving fin of a tropical fish. Her shoes were red ; there was a touch of red in the garnishing of her gloves, another in her hat.

She stepped out of the car and, turning back towards the open door, ' Well, Susan,' she said, ' you don't seem to be in any hurry to get out.'

Susan, who was bending down to pick up the parcels scattered on the floor of the car, looked up.

' I 'm just coming,' she said.

She reached hurriedly for the bunch of white roses and the terrine of *foie gras*. Reaching, she dropped the box containing the chocolate cake.

Mrs. Escobar laughed. ' You old goose,' she said, and a charming mockery set her voice deeply vibrating. ' Come out and let Robbins take the things. You 'll take them, Robbins,' she added in a different tone, turning to the chauffeur, ' you 'll take them, won't you ? '

She looked at him intimately ; her smile was appealing, almost languishing.

' Won't you, Robbins ? ' she repeated, as though she were asking the most immense of personal favours.

That was Mrs. Escobar's way. She liked to endow every relationship, the most casual, the most business-like or formal, with a certain intimate, heart-to-heart quality. She talked to shop assistants about their sweethearts, smiled at servants as though she wanted to make them her confidants or even her lovers, discussed philosophy with the plumber, gave chocolates to district messenger boys and even, when they were particularly cherubic, maternally kissed them. She wanted to 'get into touch with people,' as she called it, to finger and tweak their souls and squeeze the secrets out of their hearts. She wanted everybody to be aware of her, to like and adore her at first sight. Which did not prevent her from flying into rages with the shop assistants who could not provide her immediately with precisely the thing she wanted, from violently abusing the servants when they failed to answer the bell with a sufficient promptitude, from calling the dilatory plumber a thief and a liar, from dismissing the messenger boy who brought a present from the wrong admirer, not only chocolateless and unkissed, but without even a tip.

'Won't you?' And her look seemed to add, 'for *my* sake.' Her eyes were long and narrow. The lower lid described an almost straight horizontal line, the upper a gradual curve. Between the lids, a pair of pale blue irises rolled their lights expressively this way and that.

The chauffeur was young and new to his post. He blushed, he averted his eyes. 'Oh yes, m'm, of course,' he said, and touched his cap.

Susan abandoned the chocolate cake and the *foie gras* and stepped out. Her arms were full of parcels and flowers.

'You look like a little Mother Christmas,'

256

said Mrs. Escobar, playfully affectionate.
' Let me take something.'  She selected the
bunch of white roses, leaving to Susan the
bag of oranges, the cold roast chicken, the
tongue and the teddy bear.

Robbins opened the gate ; they stepped
into the little garden.

' Where 's Ruth ? ' said Mrs. Escobar.
' Isn't she expecting us ? ' Her voice expressed disappointment and implied reproof.
Evidently, she had expected to be met at the
gate and escorted across the garden.

' I suppose she couldn't leave Baby,' said
Susan, looking anxiously at Mrs. Escobar over
the top of her heaped-up parcels.  ' One can
never be certain of being able to do what one
wants when one 's got children, can one ? '
Still, she wished that Ruth had turned up at
the gate.  It would be dreadful if Mrs. Escobar were to think her negligent or ungrateful.
' Oh, Ruth, do come ! ' she said to herself, and
she wished so hard that she found herself
clenching her fists and contracting the muscles
of her stomach.

The fists and the abdominal muscles did
their work, for the door of the house suddenly
burst open and Ruth came running down the
steps, carrying Baby on her arm.

' I 'm so sorry, Mrs. Escobar,' she began.
' But, you see, Baby was just . . .'

Mrs. Escobar did not allow her to finish

her sentence. Momentarily clouded, her face
lit up again. She smiled, ravishingly. Her
eyelids came still closer together ; little lines
radiated out from them, a halo of charming
humour. ' Here's little Mother Christmas,'
she said, pointing at Susan. ' Loaded with
goodness knows what ! And a few poor
flowers from me.' She raised the roses to her
lips, kissed them and touched Ruth's cheek
with the half-opened flowers. ' And how's
this delicious person ? ' She took the child's
little hand and kissed it. The child looked
at her with large, grave eyes—candid and, by
reason of their candour, profoundly critical, like
the eyes of an angel on the day of judgment.

' How do you do,' he said in his solemn,
childish voice.

' Sweet pet ! ' said Mrs. Escobar and paid
no further attention to him. She was not
much interested in children. ' And you, my
dear ? ' she asked, addressing herself to Ruth.
She kissed her. She kissed her on the lips.

' Very well, thanks, Mrs. Escobar.'

Mrs. Escobar scrutinized her at arm's-
length, one hand on Ruth's shoulder. ' You
certainly look well, my dear child,' she said.
' And prettier than ever.' She thrust the
great sheaf of roses into the crook of the young
mother's unoccupied arm. ' What a sweet
little Madonna ! ' she exclaimed, and, turning
to Susan, ' Did you ever see anything more

charming ? ' she asked. Susan smiled and
nodded, rather awkwardly ; after all, Ruth
was her elder sister. 'And so absurdly,
*absurdly* young ! ' Mrs. Escobar went on.
' Why, it 's positively a *détournement de mineur*,
your being married and having a baby. Do
you know, my dear, you really look younger
than Susan. It 's a scandal.'

Embarrassed by Mrs. Escobar's point-
blank praises, Ruth blushed. And it was not
modesty alone that brought the blood to her
cheeks. This insistence on the youthfulness
of her appearance humiliated her. For it
was mostly due, this air of childishness, to her
clothes. She made her own frocks—rather
' artistic ' little affairs in brightly coloured
linens or large checks—made them in the
only way she knew how or had time to make
them : straight up and down, with a yoke
and no sleeves, to be worn over a shirt. Mono-
tonously schoolgirlish ! But what can you
do, if you can't afford to buy decent clothes ?
And her bobbed hair was dreadfully schoolgirlish too. She knew it. But again, what
could she do about that ? Let it grow ? It
would be such a trouble to keep tidy, and she
had so little time. Have it shingled ? But
she would need to get it waved as well, and it
would always have to be kept trimmed by a
good hairdresser. All that meant money.
Money, money, money !

No, if she looked so preposterously young that was simply because she was poor. Susan was a baby, five years her junior. But she looked more grown-up. She looked grown-up, because she was properly dressed in frocks from a real dressmaker. Grown-up clothes, though she was only seventeen. And her cropped brown hair was beautifully waved. Mrs. Escobar gave Susan everything she wanted. Every blessed thing.

Suddenly she found herself hating and despising this enviably happy sister of hers. After all, what was she? Just a little pet lapdog in Mrs. Escobar's house. Just a doll ; Mrs. Escobar amused herself by dressing her up, playing with her, making her say ' Mama.' It was a despicable position, despicable. But even as she thought of Susan's contemptible-ness, she was complaining to the fates which had not permitted her to share Susan's beatitude. Why should Susan have everything, when she . . . ?

But then, all at once, she remembered Baby. She turned her head impulsively and kissed the child's round, peach-pink cheek. The skin was smooth, soft and cool, like the petal of a flower. Thinking of Baby made her think of Jim. She imagined how he would kiss her when he came back from work. And this evening, while she sewed, he would read aloud from Gibbon's *Decline and Fall*. How she adored him, when he sat there in his spectacles, reading ! And the curious way he pronounced the word ' Persians '—not ' Pershuns,' but ' Perzyans.' The thought of the Perzyans made her violently wish that he were there beside her, so that she could throw her arms round his neck and kiss him. Perzyans, Perzyans—she repeated the word to herself. Oh, *how* she adored him !

With a sudden outburst of affection, intensified at once by repentance for her odious thoughts and the recollection of Jim, she turned to her sister.

' Well, Sue,' she said. They kissed over the cold roast chicken and the tongue.

Mrs. Escobar looked at the two sisters and, looking, was filled with pleasure. How charming they were, she thought ; how fresh and young and pretty ! She felt proud of them. For after all, were they not in some sort her own invention ? A couple of young girls, nicely brought up, luxuriously even ; then suddenly orphaned and left without a penny. They might simply have sunk, disappeared and never been heard of again. But Mrs. Escobar, who had known their mother, came to the rescue. They were to come and live with her, poor children ! and she would be their mother. A little ungratefully, as it always seemed to her, Ruth had preferred to accept young Jim Waterton's offer of a pre-

mature and hazardous marriage. Waterton
had no money, of course ; he was only a boy,
with all his career to make. But Ruth had
made her choice, deliberately. They had
been married nearly five years now. Mrs.
Escobar had been a little hurt. Still, she had
periodically paid her fairy godmother's visits
to Purlieu Villas ; she had stood plain human
godmother to the baby. Susan, meanwhile,
who was only thirteen when her father died,
had grown up under Mrs. Escobar's care.
She was rising eighteen now, and charming.

'The greatest pleasure in the world,' Mrs.
Escobar was fond of saying, 'is being kind
to other people.' Particularly, she might
have added, when the other people are young
and ravishing little creatures who worship you.

'Dear children,' she said, and, coming
between them, she put an arm round either's
waist. She felt all at once deeply and beautifully moved—much as she felt when she heard
the Sermon on the Mount or the story of the
woman taken in adultery read out in church.
'Dear children.' Her rich voice trembled
a little, the tears came into her eyes. She
pressed the two girls more closely to her.
Interlaced, they walked along the path towards
the door of the house. Robbins followed at
a respectful distance, carrying the *foie gras*
and the chocolate cake.

## II

'But why isn't it a train ? ' asked Baby.

'But it's such a lovely bear.'

'Such a beautiful . . .' Susan insisted.

The faces of the sisters expressed an embarrassed anxiety. Who could have foreseen it ? Baby hated the teddy bear. He wanted a train, and nothing but a train. And Mrs. Escobar had chosen the bear herself. It was a most special bear, comic in a rather artistic way, don't you know ; made of black plush, with very large eyes of white leather and boot-buttons.

'And see how it rolls,' wheedled Ruth. She gave the animal a push ; it rolled across the floor. 'On wheels,' she added. Baby had a weakness for wheels.

Susan reached out and drew the bear back again. 'And when you pull this string,' she explained, 'it roars.' She pulled the string. The bear squeaked hoarsely.

'But I want a train,' insisted the child. 'With rails and tunnels and signals.' He called them siggernals.

'Another time, my darling,' said Ruth. 'Now go and give your bear a big kiss. Poor Teddy ! He's so sad.'

The child's lips trembled, his face became distorted with grief, he began to cry. 'I want siggernals,' he said. 'Why doesn't she bring

263

me siggernals?' He pointed accusingly at Mrs. Escobar.

'Poor pet,' said Mrs. Escobar. 'He shall have his siggernals.'

'No, no,' implored Ruth. 'He really adores his bear, you know. It's just a foolish idea he's got into his head.'

'Poor *little* pet,' Mrs. Escobar repeated. But how badly brought up the child was, she thought. So spoiled, and *blasé* already. She had taken such trouble about the bear. A real work of art. Ruth ought to be told, for her own good and the child's. But she was so touchy. How silly it was of people to be touchy about this sort of thing ! Perhaps the best thing would be to talk to Susan about it and let her talk to Ruth quietly, when they were alone together.

Ruth tried to make a diversion. 'Look at this lovely book Mrs. Escobar has brought you.' She held up a brand new copy of Lear's *Book of Nonsense*. 'Look.' She turned over the pages invitingly before the child's eyes.

'Don't want to look,' Baby replied, determined to be a martyr. In the end, however, he could not resist the pictures. 'What's that?' he asked, sulkily, still trying to pretend that he wasn't interested.

'Would you like me to read you one of these lovely poems?' asked Mrs. Escobar,

heaping coals of fire on the despiser of the
bear.

' Oh yes,' cried Ruth with an anxious eager-
ness. ' Yes, please.'

' Please,' repeated Susan.

Baby said nothing, but when his mother
wanted to hand the book to Mrs. Escobar, he
tried to resist. . . . ' It 's my book,' he said
in a voice of loud and angry complaint.

' Hush,' said Ruth, and stroked his head
soothingly. He relinquished the book.

' Which shall it be ? ' asked Mrs. Escobar,
turning over the pages of the volume. ' " The
Yonghy-Bonghy-Bo " ? Or " The Pobble
who has no Toes " ? Or " The Dong " ?
Or " The Owl and the Pussy Cat " ? Which ? '
She looked up, smiling enquiringly.

' " The Pobble," ' suggested Susan.

' I think " The Owl and the Pussy Cat "
would be the best to begin with,' said Ruth.
' It 's easier to understand than the others.
You 'd like to hear about the Pussy, wouldn't
you, darling ? '

The child nodded, unenthusiastically.

' Sweet pet ! ' said Mrs. Escobar. ' He
shall have his Pussy. I love it too.' She
found her place in the book. ' " The Owl
and the Pussy Cat," ' she announced in a voice
more richly and cooingly vibrant than the
ordinary. Mrs. Escobar had studied elocu-
tion with the best teachers, and was fond

of acting, for charity. She had been un-
forgettable as Tosca in aid of the Hoxton
Children's Hospital. And then there was
her orthopaedic Portia, her tuberculous Mrs.
Tanqueray (or was Mrs. Tanqueray for the
incurables ?).

' What 's a owl ? ' asked Baby.

Interrupted, Mrs. Escobar began a preliminary reading of the poem to herself ; her
lips moved as she read.

' An owl 's a kind of big funny bird,' his
mother answered and put her arm round him.
She hoped he 'd keep quieter if she held him
like this.

' Do nowls bite ? '

' Owls, darling, not nowls.'

' Do they bite ? '

' Only when people tease them.'

' Why do people tease them ? '

' Sh-sh ! ' said Ruth. ' Now you must listen.
Mrs. Escobar 's going to read you a lovely
story about an owl and a pussy.'

Mrs. Escobar, meanwhile, had been study-
ing her poem. ' Too charming ! ' she said,
to nobody in particular, smiling as she spoke
with eyes and lips. ' Such poetry, really,
though it is nonsense. After all, what is
poetry but nonsense ? Divine nonsense.'
Susan nodded her agreement. ' Shall I
begin ? ' Mrs. Escobar enquired.

' Oh, do,' said Ruth, without ceasing to

caress the child's silky hair.   He was calmer
now.

Mrs. Escobar began :—

' " The aul and the pooseh-cut went to sea
In a beautiful (after a little pause and with intensity) *pea-grreen* boat.
They took some honey and (the rich voice rose
a tone and sank) plenty of money,
Wrapped (little pause) up (little pause) in a
five-pound note." '

' What 's a five-pound note ? ' asked Baby.
Ruth pressed her hand more heavily on the
head, as though to squeeze down his rising
curiosity.   ' Sh-sh ! ' she said.
Ignoring the interruption, Mrs. Escobar
went on, after a brief dramatic silence, to the
second stanza.

' " The aul looked up to the starrs above (her
voice thrilled deeply with the passion of
the tropical and amorous night)
And sang to a small (little pause) guitarr. . ." '

' Mummy, what 's a guit . . .? '
' Hush, pet, hush.'   She could almost feel
the child's questioning spirit oozing out
between her confining fingers.
With a green flash of emeralds, a many-
coloured glitter of brilliants, Mrs. Escobar laid
her long white hand on her heart and raised
her eyes towards imaginary constellations.

' " Oh lovely poosseh, oh poosseh my love,
What a (from high, the voice dropped emphati-
 cally) *beau*tiful poosseh you are, you are,
What a *beau*tiful poosseh you are ! " '

 ' But, mummy, do owls like cats ? '
 ' Don't talk, darling.'
 ' But you told me cats eat birds.'
 ' Not this cat, my pet.'
 ' But you said so, mummy . . .'
Mrs. Escobar began the next stanza.

' " Said the cut to the aul, You elegant faul,
How charrmingly sweet you sing (Mrs. Escobar's voice became languishing).
Come, let us be murried ; too long have we
 turried.
But *what* (pause ; Mrs. Escobar made a despairing gesture, luminous with rings)
 shall we do (pause) for the (her voice rose
 to the question) rring, the rring ?
But *what* shall we do for the rring ?

' " So they sailed away for a yeerr and a day
To the lund where the bong-tree grows. . . ." ' '

 ' What 's a bongtrygroze, mummy ? '
 Mrs. Escobar slightly raised her voice so
as to cover the childish interruption and went
on with her recitation.

' " And there (pause) in a wood (pause) a *Pig*-
 gywig stood,
With a rring . . ." ' '

' But, mummy . . .'

' " With a rring (Mrs. Escobar repeated still
more loudly, describing in the air, as she
did so, a flashing circle) at the end of his
nose, his nose . . ." '

' Mummy ! '   The child was furious with impatience ; he shook his mother's arm.   ' Why
don't you say ?   What is a bongtrygroze ? '

' You must wait, my pet.'

Susan put her finger to her lips.   ' Sh-sh ! '
Oh, how she wished that he would be good !
What would Mrs. Escobar think ?   And her
reading was so beautiful.

' " With a rring (Mrs. Escobar described a
still larger circle) at the end of his nose." '

' It 's a kind of tree,' whispered Ruth.

' " Deerr peeg, arre you willing to sell for one
shilling
Your rring ?   Said the Peeggy, I will.
So they took it a-way and were murried next day
By the turrkey who lives on the hill (the dreamy
note in Mrs. Escobar's voice made the
turkey's hill sound wonderfully blue,
romantic and remote),
By the turrkey who lives on the hill.

' " They dined on mince and slices of quince,
Which they ate with a runcible spoon,
And . . ." '

' What 's runcible ? '
' Hush, darling.'

' " . . . hand in hand (the voice became coo-
    ingly tender, bloomy like a peach with
    velvety sentiment) by the edge . . ." '

' But why do you say sh-sh, like that ? ' the
little boy shouted.   He was so angry, that he
began to hit his mother with his fists.

The interruption was so scandalous, that
Mrs. Escobar was forced to take notice of it.
She contented herself with frowning and laying
her finger on her lips.

' " . . . by the edge of the sand (all the ocean
    was in Mrs. Escobar's voice),
They danced (how gay and yet how exqui-
    sitely, how nuptially tender !) by the light
    (she spoke very slowly ; she allowed her
    hand, which she had lifted, to come gradu-
    ally down, like a tired bird, on to her knee)
    of the moo-oon." '

If any one could have heard those final
words, he would have heard interstellar space,
and the mystery of planetary motion, and
Don Juan's serenade, and Juliet's balcony.
If any one could have heard them.   But the
scream which Baby uttered was so piercingly
loud, that they were quite inaudible.

## III

' I think you ought to talk to Ruth seriously one day,' said Mrs. Escobar, on the way back from Purlieu Villas, ' about Baby. I don't think she really brings him up at all well. He 's spoiled.'

The accusation was couched in general terms. But Susan began at once to apologize for what she felt sure was Baby's particular offence.

' Of course,' she said, ' the trouble was that there were so many words in the poem he didn't understand.'

Mrs. Escobar was annoyed at having been too well understood.

' The poem ? ' she repeated, as though she didn't understand what Susan was talking about. ' Oh, I didn't mean that. I thought he was so good, considering, while I was reading. Didn't you ? '

Susan blushed, guiltily. ' I thought he interrupted rather a lot,' she said.

Mrs. Escobar laughed indulgently. ' But what can you expect of a little child like that ? ' she said. 'No, no ; I was thinking of his behaviour in general. At tea, for example. . . . You really ought to talk to Ruth about it.'

Susan promised that she would.

Changing the subject, Mrs. Escobar began to talk about Sydney Fell, who was coming to

dinner that evening. Such a darling creature !
She liked him more and more. He had a
most beautiful mouth ; so refined and sensitive, and yet at the same time so strong, so
sensual. And he was so witty and such an
accomplished amorist. Susan listened in
misery and silence.

'Don't you think so ?' Mrs. Escobar kept
asking insistently. 'Don't you think he's
delightful ?'

Susan suddenly burst out. 'I hate him,'
she said, and began to cry.

'You hate him ?' said Mrs. Escobar.
'But why ? Why ? You're not jealous, are
you ?' She laughed.

Susan shook her head.

'You are !' Mrs. Escobar insisted. 'You
are !'

Susan continued obstinately to shake her
head. But Mrs. Escobar knew that she had
got her revenge.

'You silly, silly child,' she said in a voice
in which there were treasures of affection.
She put her arm round the girl's shoulders,
drew her gently and tenderly towards her and
began to kiss her wet face. Susan abandoned
herself to her happiness.

Printed in Great Britain by T. and A. CONSTABLE LTD.
at the University Press, Edinburgh